Ten Commandments for Kissing Gloria Jean

Ten
Commandments
for Kissing
Gloria Jean

By Britt Leigh

Pauline
BOOKS & MEDIA
Boston

Library of Congress Cataloging-in-Publication Data

Leigh, Britt.
  Ten commandments for kissing Gloria Jean / by Britt Leigh.
    pages cm
  Summary: While trying to navigate the world of dating and attend Confirmation class,
fourteen-year-old Gloria Jean discovers that she has celiac disease.
  Includes bibliographical references.
  ISBN-13: 978-0-8198-7491-7
  ISBN-10: 0-8198-7491-4
  [1. Dating (Social customs)--Fiction. 2. Celiac disease--Fiction. 3. Catholics--Fiction.] I. Title.
  PZ7.L53295Te 2014
  [Fic]--dc23

                              2013024734

Scripture texts in this work are taken from the *New American Bible, Revised Edition* © 2010, 1991,
1986, 1970 Confraternity of Christian Doctrine, Washington, D.C. and are used by permission of
the copyright owner. All rights reserved. No part of the *New American Bible* may be reproduced in
.any form without permission in writing from the copyright owner.

Excerpts from the English translation of the *Catechism of the Catholic Church* for use in the United
States of America, copyright © 1994, United States Catholic Conference, Inc. — Libreria Edi-
trice Vaticana. Used with permission.

White Blank Page
Words and Music by Mumford & Sons
Copyright © 2009 UNIVERSAL MUSIC PUBLISHING LTD.
All Rights in the U.S. and Canada Controlled and Administered by UNIVERSAL – POLYGRAM
INTERNATIONAL TUNES, INC.
All rights reserved. Used by permission. Reprinted by permission of Hal Leonard Corporation.

Your Love Is Extravagant
Written by Darrell Evans
Copyright © 1998 Integrity's Hosanna! Music (ASCAP) (adm. at EMICMGPublishing.com).
International copyright secured. All rights reserved. Used by permission.

Cover photo © istockphoto.com, Klubovy/Lukasz Laska
Cover design by Mary Joseph Peterson, FSP

Published by Pauline Books & Media, 50 Saint Pauls Avenue, Boston, MA 02130-3491

Printed in the USA.

www.pauline.org

Pauline Books & Media is the publishing house of the Daughters of St. Paul, an international
congregation of women religious serving the Church with the communications media.

1 2 3 4 5 6 7 8 9   17 16 15 14

For Mom and Dad,

who gave me life and love;

for Amy and Mallory,

who live it;

for all who seek the Truth

in life and love.

"It is easy to find truth;
it is hard to face it,
and harder still to follow it."

— *Fulton J. Sheen*

"We cannot give our hearts to God
and keep our bodies for ourselves."

— *Elisabeth Elliott*

I

Thou shalt
ignore the pimple
on my lip.

1

It is 6:47 p.m., and I, Gloria Jean Wisnewski, am late for my first-ever date. And I have a pimple on my lip. A pimple! On. My. *Lip*!

I gaze out the window of Mom's sedan so I don't have to look at her. It's all her fault. The being late part, not the pimple part. All her fault because she could not get the bread and shampoo before 6:00 tonight or on any one of the other three weekly trips she makes to All-Mart. It just had to be the very night I am going to the movies when Connor Riley will be there. Connor Riley, who's the cutest, nicest boy in the whole school.

In the side-view mirror, I catch a glimpse of the white bump. It looks like it's wearing a red inner tube. "Warning: objects in mirror may appear bigger than they are." This little reminder from the car is not comforting. While my lips aren't exactly full and juicy, I've been told they do curve into a sweet smile. And now that's wrecked. I groan and slump into my seat. Actually, the pimple *is* Mom's fault. She forgot to get my zit cream.

"Could you hurry up? We're already so late!" I lean forward as if I'm playing some motion-sensor video game and my body is the controller, demanding the car move forward.

Mom takes a deep breath. "Relax. You're fine." She pulls into the left lane to turn into the Sable Palms Cineplex. "I'm fine," she says under her breath.

And we've just missed the green light for our turn. Great.

Mom faces me and places her hand on mine. "Now, Gloria Jean, this is your first boy-girl party. Unsupervised. Remind me who's going to be there again."

"The birthday girl, of course. And Melissa. And Zack and Eric and Connor." I say the last part really fast.

Eden's been my best friend for years and years, and we met Melissa and the boys when we all started sixth grade at Panther Run Middle School. Usually birthday parties are just the girls or just the guys. But now that we're in eighth grade, Eden wants to get some dating practice in before high school, when everyone's dating, or so says her older sister, Sarai. So when her mom asked what she wanted to do this year, she came up with the idea of a boy-girl party at the movies so she could go on an official date with her almost-boyfriend, Zack; Melissa could go on a date with this boy she's had a crush on, Eric; and I could go on a date with Connor, who was such a gentleman that he formally asked me out at the end of sixth period. The official birthday party for just us girls to celebrate was actually a couple of weeks ago. We went to the mall and then slept over at Eden's and had a fashion show with the new outfits we bought for tonight. We like to plan ahead.

Eden and I were meant to be best friends. Evidence #1: we both have fall birthdays so, thanks to school calendar rules, we have always been the oldest girls in our grade. It's one of the few times a rule is kind of cool. This one makes us *mature*.

Mom is spending this never-ending light thinking. Her mouth twists from side to side, as if she's trying to roll around the various tones she can use before settling on the one that feels right. "I hear from Eden's mom that she's been spending lots of time with Zack. Like they're dating." She looks at the traffic light. Then at me. "You know how your father and I feel about dating." She squeezes my hand. "We don't think you're old enough. But what do you think about all this?" Her pitch gets higher, along with her eyebrows.

I nudge her hand off mine. It's not quite the one I want to hold tonight. I look at her square in the face. "I think I'm ready. You let J.P. date when he was sixteen. What's two years?"

Mom slowly nods. "A lot," she says in a restrained voice. "But even with your brother, he had to start with group things with friends."

"Right! So this is not a *date*." I smile wide. Maybe she gets it! Maybe I can tell her! I'd been kind of scared to share what I was really hoping for tonight. Afraid she'd say no to me going. "We're all just hanging out. It's a movie. We won't even be talking."

Mom purses her lips and then turns away from me and focuses on the stoplight. "Exactly. At your age, sometimes kids go to movies so they can kiss. Especially at these romantic comedy type of movies." She darts a look at me, then goes back to her staring contest with the traffic light.

I don't know how Mom knows this stuff, but yes, I would like Connor Riley to go out with me and kiss me. That fact is entirely the reason Eden and I picked this movie, *Fairly Able*. Well, not entirely. The winner of our favorite fashion show, *Tres Chic*, designed some of the wardrobe for it. "Mo-om!" I blush and put my hands on my face. This is the longest. Light. EVER.

"Okay, okay." Mom lifts her hands from the steering wheel for a minute. She turns back to me with a simpering smile and brushes the side bang off my forehead. "You girls will stay together, then." Uh-oh. This means one thing. She misheard my tone of voice and still thinks I don't get it or worse that I don't *want* to get it, yet.

"Green light, Mom!" Finally, finally! I bounce up so I can catch a glimpse of Connor waiting for me on the steps.

Connor is not the type to get pimples on his lips. He has perfect, peachy-tan skin and full, juicy, red lips. It amazes me how boys can get lips like that without liner, gloss, and special lipsticks made with chemical plumping agents. He is soooo adorable. I swoon back into my seat.

The sedan rolls into the horseshoe lane in front of the theater steps. Mom puts the car into park. She tucks the ever-loose section of hair behind my ear. "I'm so glad you haven't asked me about destroying your hair with those dyes yet—maybe if next time we curl it. . . ."

I unbuckle my seat belt and peck her on the cheek. I can't take one more minute of this. It is also all her fault that I have what I call dirty-dishwater blonde hair. Not rich, mahogany brown hair like Connor Riley has. Or always-shiny, auburn hair like Eden has. Nope, Mom and I are, as she likes to call it, *hair twins*.

"Gotta go," I tell Mom as I slide out the door. "I see Connor on the top step."

"Where are Eden and Melissa?" Mom calls through the window.

"Must be inside already," I say and tap the car like it's a horse to get it going.

I skip up the steps. "Hi, Connor," I say. Suddenly my sandals and the pedicure Eden gave me seem really interesting.

"Hi, Gloria Jean," Connor says.

His brown, boat-style shoes must be really interesting, too.

"My mom made me wear this," he says, gesturing up and down his khakis and navy blue polo. Then he grins that grin that made me fall in like with him. It starts slow and then widens to one side.

I laugh. And I'm thankful that my outfit is not anyone's fault. It is perfect. I am wearing a deep magenta top with a little peek-hole over a white tank top; a turquoise skirt with magenta piping at the bottom; and strappy, choco-late-colored sandals. Eden thought the skirt looked weird on the hanger, but "gor-*geous*" during the fashion show.

"Your eyes match your skirt," Connor says.

I look at him quizzically. My eyes are not turquoise. They are pale blue, like dirty watercolor water, pale blue.

"My brothers told me to say that," he says. He looks at our feet again.

Connor has two older brothers—twins. They're seven-teen, so I can't tell if they wanted to be helpful or were teasing. Maybe he means my eyes are pretty. I crane my head so I can look into his eyes. "Thanks. I like your eyes, too."

And it's the truth. He has dark, chocolate-brown eyes. How am I out with Connor Riley, the most perfect guy in the whole eighth grade class at Panther Run Middle? Especially when I, Gloria Jean Wisnewski, have a pimple on my lip!

Connor straightens up. "I already got the tickets. Zack and Eric are already inside with everyone else. Wanna go in?"

I nod. "I'll get the popcorn, soda, and candy. If you want, I mean."

When J.P. dated a girl he met at college this past sum-mer, Dad always told him to bring extra money, because true gentlemen always paid, even if the girl offered.

"Cool," Connor says.

Uh-oh. Maybe he is not a true gentleman.

We go inside and get the snacks. We find our theater. Not once does he open a door. Oh dear. He is not a true gentleman.

Inside the small theater, I see Eden close with Zack in the very top row. She waves and motions down, meaning we shouldn't sit with them. I don't see Melissa anywhere. So I lead us to two open seats on the aisle. It's a two-hour and twenty-minute show. I foresee needing to be close to an aisle or door, especially with the jumbo-sized soda Connor suggested we get, you know, so we could share. But he walks to the smack-dab middle of the row and pats on a cushion. Then, when I try to put the soda in the cup-holder, he shakes his head and lifts the armrest.

I giggle. I place the popcorn in between us and settle back. The lights darken. Good, he can't see the pimple anymore. Not that I think he's thinking about it, because now he's putting his arm around my shoulders. He is defi-nitely *not* a true gentleman. But this time it's a good thing! Cause I think that means there's a chance he'll kiss me, even if it is only the first date.

Suddenly, a warm, tingly feeling zaps around the back of my neck and up to the backs of my earlobes, like I've been caught texting in class and the teacher is going to read it out loud, even though I know it's not actually any-thing embarrassing. Now that I am actually here on this date, I realize that of course it feels very different being on a date than how I feel when just seeing a couple dating on TV or hearing about Eden's dates with Zack. I twist around and try to find her. Her eye catches mine and she glares and softly juts her head toward Connor. He's clearing his throat and looking at the screen. I look too. Just some ad-vertisements for a dental service and fun (not really) facts about movies I haven't seen.

I can feel him subtly shift in his seat. He's looking at me! I shift a little so our hips make a vee. I take a sip of soda and hope that the cold of the ice somehow makes it to my flushing neck and cheeks.

"Sooo . . . what'd you . . . do . . . this week?" Connor asks. His brothers must not have told him anything else about talking about on dates.

"Oh, you know, school. I'm thinking of entering that fashion design contest they talked about during closing announcements. Are you planning to enter the other one, the boat contest?"

"Nah, I don't think I will. Not my thing."

"Ah." I wonder what his Thing is. For the past two years he's been this boy who answers questions in class, but not too much, so he's not annoying like this guy I just met last night in Confirmation class. And Connor gets them wrong sometimes, but not too much, so he's not like Eric, who thinks sounding like an idiot is funny and actually did a book report on a series of little kid books full of fart jokes. No, Connor is always nice, if unreadable. Kind of like a cat in that way.

He doesn't say anything for the longest five seconds.

"Well, last night I had my first Confirmation class," I say. I hope that doesn't sound too boring or churchy. But I need to say something about this week that is new to him. We are in three of the same classes. Boys.

"Oh, cool. I started mine last week," Connor says. He takes a slurp of soda. "Didn't know you went." He stares ahead at the screen.

I didn't know he went either! Maybe Mom will be more

chill about this whole dating thing if she knows Connor is Catholic, too. Then again, I don't exactly want to come off as a nun wannabe! There's a girl in my Confirmation class who knows SO MUCH it's a little scary. I take some popcorn. "Yeah. We go to Saint Jose Maria Escriva. It's kind of a drive. But I'm so ready to start finally. I had to miss a bunch of classes last year, so they told me to re-do Year One."

"Same with me." Another slurp of soda. "My mom forgot about registration. We don't even go to church all that much anymore . . . just Christmas and Easter," Connor says. "I don't get the big deal . . . all that Holy Spirit stuff, you know?"

I crunch my popcorn thoughtfully. I try to nod sympathetically. But the answer is no, I do not really know. Mom, Dad, J.P., and I have always gone to church every Sunday. J.P. was even an altar server for a bit. The older kids who man the tables after Mass trying to get us to sign up for activities seem nice and happy. I want to tell him I get the big deal. Sort of.

"Well, Mrs. Fermacelli, my religious ed teacher, said Confirmation means you're given all these graces to help you now that you're a fully initiated Catholic. Sort of like a *Bat Mitzvah*," I tell him.

"A what kind of bat?" Connor asks.

"*Bat Mitzvah*. The thing at the synagogue Eden had last year. You were there."

"Oh yeah! That was one mad party. That's cool." He slurps his soda again. At this rate, I am not so concerned about being in the middle of the aisle.

I am concerned that his arm is around me, but he is not looking at me. Maybe it's all the church talk. I switch back to school stuff. "Sooo . . . this term project Mr. Gio's making us do. You're with Eric, right?"

He nods. The term project is this big thing our social studies teacher, Mr. Giopolous, is making us do in pairs. We have to present the cultural history of a subject using modern technology, like podcasts or apps. Of course, Eden and I are together. We haven't picked our topic yet.

"He said something about soccer . . . ," I say to get him started on *some* kind of trail, otherwise this conversation is trailing off . . .

Connor's eyes widen, and I can see them catch a glint of light from the screen. It seems I have hit a Thing. "Oh yeah," he starts all excitedly.

I let him talk about sports until the movie starts and let him keep slurping the soda as long as he keeps letting his arm rest along the back of my neck, which is feeling significantly less electrified.

Then, halfway through the movie, I am desperately wishing we were on the aisle and not in the middle. And it's not from too much of the soda that Connor has finished by himself. Oh no. It's the Troubles.

2

I squirm on the theater seat. No no no no no not now. Maybe I can hold it. Everyone laughs at something the little dog does on-screen. It covers up the sound of my stomach. Nope.

I stand up, then crouch down when someone whisper-yells "Hey!" from the back of the theater. I start crawling over Connor.

"What's wrong?" Connor says in a husky voice.

Oooh, that sounds manly, but *sooo* not important right now. "It's ok . . . just gotta . . . excuse me . . . I'll be right back." Thinking quickly, I grab the nearly-empty cup. "Gonna get more soda."

"*Shhh!*" the lady next to Connor says.

"Sorry," I whisper. And then sorry again because I have to squeeze past her legs and everyone else's so I can high-tail it to the ladies' room.

If Connor thinks this is weird and doesn't want to kiss me, then this is all Poppa's fault. Poppa gets the Troubles, too. A lot. I used to think it was because he was old, but Mom says Gigi never had them, not even before she died, "God rest her soul," and she always teased Poppa about them. Mom says her parents had a relationship where they could talk about anything, and that was a good thing. It was even cute sometimes, she'd say. Well, it is not cute when the Troubles have cost me

* the last seventeen minutes of my geography test;

* the ability to go to beaches without, how shall I say it, *facilities*, for long stretches of time, which is difficult, seeing as I live on the east coast of Florida;

* the roller coaster ride at Disney World because Mom said quite loudly near the cute ride attendant, "Are you *sure* you want to go, knowing how 'sensitive' you're feeling?"; and

* quite possibly, the chance to kiss Connor Riley.

When I get back fourteen minutes later, everything in the plot is wrong. The guy isn't with the girl anymore, the dog is sad, and the music isn't happy. "What'd I miss?" I whisper into Connor's ear.

"Oh," he starts. He snakes his arm around my neck. "Well, um, first—"

"SHHH!" the lady says.

"Never mind. I'll tell you later. Wasn't much." Connor pulls back his arm and starts trying to grab for a straw.

Oops. The soda.

"Where's the soda?" he asks.

I smack my forehead. "Oops. I got it, but then stopped by the bathroom and must have forgotten it on the counter." I wince. "Probably too gross to get it now," I say in a small, lame voice. Now I'm sure that weird feeling at the back of my neck has spread all around my face.

He looks at me funny. "Uh, okay. Yeah. Too gross." He doesn't put his arm back.

We sit like that for the rest of the movie. When the guy and the girl are back together, the dog's wearing a sombrero and winking, and the happy music brings the screen to the credits, Connor and I leave.

Eden and Zack are waiting on the steps outside. They are holding hands. "Where's Melissa at?" I ask.

"She and Eric went to a different movie," Eden says. "Then she texted me that she left early. Hey! There's my mom!" She squeezes Zack's hand really hard.

Then it's just the three of us. Zack looks at Connor and raises an eyebrow. Connor gives the slightest little shrug. Zack gives a lopsided wave. "Gonna go bug my brother for a ride. He works around here. See ya." He bounds down the steps toward the shops in the plaza.

And then it's just the two of us.

"I had fun!" I say a little too brightly.

"Yeah, me, too." Connor looks at a poster for an upcoming action movie.

"You want to go see that?" I ask. Should I say "with me"?

He shrugs. "Maybe."

We walk down a couple of steps and stop. This is getting a little awkward.

"Hey, isn't that your mom's car?" Now it's getting a *lot* awkward.

"Yeah," I say.

"Okay. Well, bye." Then. He. HUGS. Me. And walks back to the side of the building.

I run down the steps and get into the car.

Connor Riley did not kiss me, and it is not at all the pimple's fault. Or at all Mom's fault. Or all his fault, really. No, it was all the Troubles' fault.

II

Thou shalt brush thy teeth.

3

I sit in the bathroom until it's obvious I won't have a repeat of earlier tonight. Dad harrumphs to the bathroom door and calls out, "This thing is buzzing and blinking and going bananas." Something clacks on the tile. Once he lumbers away, I crack open the door. Eden's sent like fifteen texts. My phone is like a manic robot. I set it beside the sink. Will address *that* in a minute. But first I want to clear my head, and somehow I think washing my face will accomplish that.

Beads of water and liquid foundation roll over my lips and spill to the sink below. I take a towel and rub my face until it is red and blotchy. Great, now Mom will think I've been crying. I lock the door. My back has started insanely itching. This is not the first time, and I've learned better than to scratch. I climb into the tub, hoping maybe the cool porcelain will calm it down.

Earlier today, during our sixth period class, Eden had instructed me to call her the minute I got home from the party-date. The minute I got home, I was, as my Dad likes to say, *indisposed*. I looked it up once. It means "slightly ill." But the second definition is "averse," which means to really dislike something. So for extra credit for life's vocabulary homework, I am indisposed to tell Eden about what happened, I mean *didn't* happen, on the date that wasn't even supposed to be a date. I take a deep breath before calling her.

"You're back!" I have to hold the phone away from my ear, she squees so loud. "Sooooo, how was the kiss? Tell me! How long did it last? Was it . . . French?" You can almost hear the ooh-la-la in her voice.

Eden has been kissed before. A dozen times. Eden was also the first among us to become a woman. And not just because she had her *Bat Mitzvah* first, if you know what I mean. And I think you do.

I press my lips together. I'm still not ready for the third degree. On the way home, Mom wouldn't let Dad turn the radio up, and she kept sneaking looks at me, like she expected me to be full of news about the party. I distracted myself by staring out the window. What could I use here? I open the shampoo bottle and let a little of the pearly white goop drizzle onto the rim of the tub. "No," I whisper.

I look over the edge of the tub. Yup, door's still locked.

"Oh, well, that's okay. That means he's a gentleman. Probably saving it for the next date." Evidence #2 that Eden and I are meant to be best friends: she always tries to make me feel better.

"Yeah. Maybe." I use my finger to shape the white glob into a triangle. Then I get the body wash with beads— the good kind we use for guests—and smear that into a square atop my shampoo skirt.

"What's with you? You don't seem excited at all."

"I dunno. It just wasn't what I hoped it would be." The not-a-date date. Why wasn't I saying "the date"? Eden thinks I mean the kiss. "I don't think he likes me very much."

"That's like so impossible, Glorie Jeanie. You're the most likable person I know."

I make a little jacket with the pale yellow shower-gel. "Thanks. He liked my skirt, at least."

"See! That skirt you picked out at the mall? Good call! And you were so right about the sundress I picked out. I kept having to pull it up all last night. You should like be my personal shopper from now on."

Ever since we were little kids, Eden's been the color-ful one—as bright as the rolls of fabric in my favorite craft shop. Everyone was always talking to her. One day her mom threw her a Pretty Princess party "just because." But I think it was because her dad, who's divorced from her mom and living an hour away, couldn't take her on his weekends for three straight months. Anyway, I picked out the pinkest dress and made my own crown. Every girl there started talking to me about my dress and asking for help with theirs. It became a fun challenge—see if I could get noticed just as myself even though Eden was there. When we met Melissa two years ago in homeroom, she warmed to Eden's bubbly talk and gushed about her first-day-of-school outfit. Which I picked out.

"Only if you pay me." I consider the little outfit I just designed with the bath products. It'd look good on Eden. I smooth two of the edges out to make straps for her. "Sorry I didn't call right away."

"It's cool. I was actually just texting Zack. I think I'm ready to give him the Pajama Test. Mom and Sarai are going to go shopping for her homecoming dress tomorrow after synagogue, so I'll have the house to myself."

Zack was kisses eight through at least a dozen. Eden conducts the Pajama Test only when she thinks she wants to get serious about a guy. "Oooh. I think you should wear the black and hot-pink argyle PJs."

"Hmmm . . . I dunno. The pants are cute. Buuuut . . ."

I know immediately what she's worried about. "Just don't wear the button-down shirt. You don't want to be too matchy-matchy. Want me to bring over my black V-neck top?"

"Oh, yes, totally! Thanks so much! Oh, and after you hide in the closet during the Test, we can have brunch."

"Yes! So, you think he'll pass?"

"He just might. Okay, Mom's yammering away at me. See you tomorrow, 11:30?"

"See you then!"

"Byeeeeee!"

I sigh and sink back into the edge of the tub. I'm not quite ready to face the excited eyes and eager questions of Mom and Dad.

The movie we saw, *Fairly Able*, is a "fresh re-telling of the classic fairytale romances," according to the throaty-voice movie commercial guy. I think about this one part I did get to see. It was after I got back from the bathroom and Connor was ignoring me. The diplomat's son was yelling, "Raquel, Raquel, let down your fair hair!" The movie wants you to swoon and hope for the rescue that will come.

But now I'm thinking if I were Raquel, I'd have a choice. I could let a smarmy, too-perfect teeth guy all up in my turret, or I could start a clothing line of "fresh, classic romance, fairy-tale-inspired dresses." And true to the movie's title, Raquel is able to do both.

Tonight, the fairy tale has let me down. I feel like I'm Raquel's best friend who slept all the time. Only I won't hold my breath waiting for the handsome prince to wake me with a kiss. I feel like it's *never* going to happen. But according to Ms. Jean-Baptiste, our English teacher, anticipation is the best part. She used the example of this poem "Ode on a Grecian Urn," which is all about this piece of pottery that has this couple about to kiss painted on it. All I can think of is what it must be like, frozen in time and never getting that kiss. Your lips forever puckered like a fish. I tried it for the twelve minutes I was indisposed at home. It really hurts.

When I get out of here, I'm gonna put on my rain boots and stomp on my princess DVD collection for a while.

"Gloria Jean, sweetheart, before you head to bed, come tell us about the party." Mom's trilling yell from the living room reverberates around the tile wall of the bathroom. How does she do that?

I uncurl myself out of the tub and emerge from the bathroom.

"Again?" Mom says. She closes down an email screen from the computer in the family room. "I'll call Dr. Yam on Monday and tell her the new diet isn't working." She opens up her datebook.

"As long as she's got Trouble at home, not at her first boy-girl party, right, String Bean?" Dad beams over his paper.

Right, Dad. I fling myself on the couch. Irritable bowel syndrome is just the latest diagnosis my pediatrician has come up with. Like a fashion designer, every season she comes out with a new disease to show me, like a collection. And so far, not one has fit skinny, itty-bitty me. Well, there was this one test that was looking for a couple of antigens, whatever those are, but she said since I didn't have the magic number of two, I didn't have to worry. Mom looks back at me and frowns. Her eyes well up.

I sit forward and make direct eye contact. "It's not like last year. I promise." I stand up. "Can I just go to bed? Please? I'm going over to Eden's tomorrow morning for brunch."

Mom nods and mouths okay. Then she wriggles her shoulders to shake off the bad memory. "But we want to hear about your night!" Mom now protests in her trilling voice. "You didn't say anything in the car."

"I told you we both shouldn't have gone to get her," Dad says. He looks at me. Suddenly he does a double take. "Oh. Oh!" He folds up his paper. "I see! Dear ole dad has a mute button effect." He gets off the couch and makes a pouty face. He rests a hand on my shoulder. "Click." He slooowly starts walking away.

Mom looks at me eager-eyed.

"I'll tell you tomorrow, okay? I promise. I really am tired."

"Both of us?" Dad has shuffled back into the living room. Now he is eager-eyed.

My neck is tingling. There's no way I can get around both of them. "How 'bout Mom gives you the recap?"

Dad picks up the paper and lightly swats the armrest. "Deal!" He settles back into his spot and extends the foot-rest.

Mom pulls a book off the counter and goes to the couch. She snuggles up against Dad's shoulder. "Oh, all right." Then she holds the book up to the side of her face. "As soon as you get back from Eden's we'll have that girl talk," she adds in a stage whisper.

I'm glad my parents had fun on my first date. Maybe I should tell Eden the truth. She could tell me what I did wrong. Or what Connor did wrong and how to train him.

4

The next morning, Eden goops sticky, strawberry-colored, glitter-gloss around her lips.

"I thought the point of the Pajama Test was to look sick," I say.

Eden's eyes widen in the mirror. "You're so right. Here, hand me a tissue."

I swipe a box off her nightstand and get off her bed to give it to her. As I pass by, I tousle her hair. "Want to make it look really real, right?" I giggle.

Eden giggles, too. "You're the best." She pulls me to her side and rests her head on my shoulder. In the mirror,

I see her contemplating the picture of us. She squeezes my side. "Maybe one day soon, I'll be helping you get messy for *Connor's* Pajama Test, and we'll both have boyfriends at the same time."

I put my head on hers. "I'd like that." Because, truthfully, once Zack passes the Pajama Test, Eden will be out of this picture, and I'll be stuck looking at my lips in the mirror alone. Hopefully zit-free. I scowl at the thing. I swear it grew half an inch overnight.

The doorbell rings. "He's here!"

"Act the part!" I whisper.

"He's here," Eden half-growls, half-coughs.

We dash into the front room. I hide in the vacuum closet and Eden takes a big sniffle and opens the door.

"Hi," she says weakly.

"Hi," Zack says. "So you're sick."

Eden coughs. "Yeah, a little."

"You look it," Zack says.

"Gee, thanks."

"No, I mean, you don't look like you usually do."

"And how's that?"

Through the slat of the closet door I can see Eden fake-shyly arch her back inward a little and trace circles on the floor with her big toe. She's got two inches on me, and some curves already. This move looks incredibly complicated, like yoga, but flirty. I wonder if I can pull that off in my new sandals.

"Pretty." Zack is blushing.

"Aww, thank youb." After three Pajama Tests, Eden has the sick voice down.

"Here, I brought this."

"Chicken soup," she says extra loud, for my benefit. "You shouldn't have."

"My mom thought it'd be nice. And I did, too," he adds quickly. "She made a lot, so we can have lunch together, if you want."

Eden runs a hand through her hair. "So you don't care that I look and sound mismerbuhbull?"

"You're not that bad." Zack inches closer toward Eden.

"You're such a good boy. But I really should get back to bed."

"There's nothing else I can do? Kiss it to make it better?"

"That's for boo-boos." Eden lightly swats Zack's arm. "So?"

And then he kisses her. And then it hits me. Why I can't tell Eden about my time with Connor. Because all along I know in the back of my head that this is all so unfair. To see if boys really like her for her, Eden just pretends to be sick. And she gets kisses. I actually *am* sick and I get the crummy date.

My breath is hot in the dark closet. I would push out the accordion-style door, but that would ruin Eden's moment. Even though he falls for things easily, Zack is a gentleman, bringing her soup, and he passed the test, so he deserves his A.

Finally, I hear the front door close. Eden swings open the closet door.

"So, did he pass?" My lying voice is nowhere near as good as Eden's sick voice. She knows I saw and heard.

"Uhh . . . um . . ."

"What? He was so perfectly sweet with the soup."

Eden bites her lip. "It . . . I . . . He was sooo close!" Her face crumples behind her hands. "But that was the worst kiss I've ever had!" she muffles.

"Why? Too much tongue? Too little tongue?" I don't actually know what I'm saying, but she's mentioned it so many times before.

"No, no. It was . . . I could taste the onion and bacon and cheese from his breakfast on his breath!" Eden walks into the kitchen and grabs a bottle of water from the fridge. She gargles right over the sink.

"So?" As soon as I say the word, I want to stuff it right back into my mouth, because really, my lips are like Fort Knox and shouldn't have let that get out.

The mascara Eden smudged under her eyelids to look wan starts to smear. "So? Not only was it nasty tasting and smelling, but, I . . . I'm *kosher*!"

Ohhhhh. Eden's mom has been encouraging her and her sister to be more observant ever since their *Bat Mitzvahs*. Skipping synagogue for the movie last night was a special treat. I guess she's taking it really seriously if she can't even have that teeny-tiny amount of meat and cheese from someone else.

Eden opens the bag of pancake mix with such force that white powder explodes everywhere. Then she part-hiccups, part-sobs, and part-laughs. "Listen to me. Look at this. Ugh."

I unravel a yard of paper towels from the roll and wet them. I hand them to her, and she starts mopping powder off her face.

"Aw. Well, maybe he was just so excited to see you and make you feel better that he forgot to brush his teeth. Maybe he's walking home right now smelling his breath in his hand and feeling really stupid and hoping he gets just one more chance."

Eden pouts. "You think so?"

"He showed he was nice enough when he passed your Pajama Test. And I bet if you told him how important it was to you that he follow the food rules, he'd do it. Remember in the movie, Cella's boyfriend became vegetarian for her and cooked her that romantic dinner of pumpkin ravioli?" I don't say it, but I think she understands that I mean she should be nice enough to give him another chance and forgive him.

"You're so right." She wads more paper towels and starts mopping the powder off the kitchen floor. "Man, that should be the number one rule of kissing, though. Always brush your teeth!"

I laugh, but my stomach feels like it has its own paper towel lump lodged inside. Connor and I had both brushed our teeth.

* * *

In the afternoon, Mom curls up on the couch with me. Dad makes a big show of getting out of the way. "I'm going to go wash the car!" he says brightly.

Mom at least rolls her eyes. I give her a general run down. To tell her the whole plot of the movie and include the part I missed while I was in the bathroom, I use some bits from a spoiler I had read online at Eden's. I also lie and tell her that Melissa, Eden, and I did sit together the whole time. I refuse to tell her about getting sick in the theater. For as long as I can remember I've had the Troubles, so practically all my life I've been put on diet after diet, had so much blood drawn I started referring to the lab tech as Mr. Vampire. The worst thing is that there hasn't been any clear answer about how to stop the Troubles. If I tell Mom how bad they're getting, there will be new rules just when I've gotten used to the ones I follow now.

Mom asks a lot of questions about Connor and Zack and this Eric boy, whom she hasn't met yet. For every other birthday party I've ever been to, she always made sure to drop me off personally and introduce herself to the parent on duty and have new kids pointed out to her. Did they come from good people, she wondered, whatever that means. I guess now that we're getting older, she can't check things out like she used to and needs to get creative to get the lowdown. I give her one-word answers. She acts like it's okay and mentions that J.P. was similarly quiet around my age. I was just a kid then. But now, as Eden keeps reminding me, we're becoming women. I wonder if he didn't want to talk with Mom because she's a girl or because she's Mom. Maybe he'd have some advice about Connor.

Later that night, J.P. makes his weekly call home from college upstate. I hover around Mom and Dad in the living room, hoping to get a chance to talk, but he only talks to them for five minutes before hanging up. Something about a football game. Great.

I'm still thinking about everything the next morning at Mass, which is in Latin. A few years ago, our church started offering the traditional Latin Mass—not sure why they call it the "extraordinary form"—at the mid-morning time slot. Mom was really excited because Gigi used to talk about it all the time, but could never find one. J.P. and I were *not* excited because we didn't even know what anyone was saying. Latin is a dead language, right?

And that's not the only thing different. People dress up more—my dad wears ties, which he doesn't even do for work! And women and girls are supposed to cover their heads. So, most people use this thing called a chapel veil, which is actually really pretty, Mom made tea one afternoon and we shopped online for ours. A couple of weeks later, she made tea again and presented me with the one I liked the most, the one made with real white lace that at first she had said was too expensive. And the music, which is some chant from the middle ages or something, sounds better than the warbling cantor at the other Mass we used to go to—even if I can't understand all the words. Anyway, it feels more mystical.

During the Gospel reading, I can see that everyone, including my Confirmation classmates, is paying attention. I look in my missal, which is a book for Mass, not a weapon. One more thing to add to life's vocabulary worksheet. Today's reading comes from Luke, chapter 16. One verse sticks out: "'The person who is trustworthy in very small matters is also trustworthy in great ones; and the person who is dishonest in very small matters is also dishonest in great ones.'"

Father Mazi starts his homily, in English, thank goodness, on honesty and not bearing false witness, one of the commandments. It seems so simple—a set of ten basic rules that tell you how to live. Eden and I are familiar with other kinds of "top-tens." We have downloaded tons of apps that list the rules for dating and how to get that first kiss. I really thought Connor and I were following them. We both dressed up. We went to a movie. He put his arm around my shoulders. But I lied to Mom about why the group really went out together. And I lied about the soda to Connor. And Eden lied about being sick. Maybe the first rule of kissing is that you shouldn't lie.

III

Thou shalt
not chew gum.

5

All anyone can talk about Monday at school is how Melissa Sanchez nearly choked on gum at the movies on Friday, and someone's grandpa skipped over three rows of seats to give her the Heimlich. Like Connor, Eric did not text his date back. Melissa buries her face in her hands after repeating the story for the fourth time in the locker room before first-period gym. There is a special place in purgatory for whoever decided that fifty teenage girls should run around and get sweaty first thing in the morning in front of fifty teenage boys just ten yards away doing their gym class. I know the expression is supposed to use the word "hell," but I'll save that for the day they make us shower in the grungy locker rooms.

Eden rubs Melissa's back and tells her in a Mom-ish voice that she'll forge a note saying Melissa can't dress out today. Melissa just sobs and the whole rickety bench shakes with her. I turn around and use this moment to quickly change my shirt. I woke up with another weird icky rash on my back, and while I know we're beyond the cooties stage, it's still gross.

I've got my gym shirt on and am half strangling myself with the crook of my elbow to get my regular tee off in a move called the shirt shimmy. The first day of school, all of the girls stood around, holding our Panther Run shirts and shorts. No one wanted to change, which Coach Nuñez calls dressing out. I thought back to this book I'd read when I was little, that described a maneuver to change shirts without letting your skin show. I tried it out. Soon all the girls were copying me. Except one.

Coach Nuñez emerges from her little office. At 6'1 and full of muscle, you can believe immediately that she once was in the Army. Even her skin is this perfect mix of the sand and field drab colors that make up camouflage. "No need to dress out today, ladies. We're all meeting in the gym to start a special unit." She looks over at me. "But I appreciate your readiness, Wisnewski."

Coach's sneakers squeak across the floor to Melissa. "You all right Sanchez?"

Melissa shakes her head and whimpers.

"What is it today?"

"Code red?" someone who just walked in suggests.

Coach Nuñez rolls her eyes, both at our class's little code system and at the issue. "Just see the nurse."

Another shake of the head. But this time her eyes meet Coach's.

"Oh, child. What is it this time? A code black?" She fakes a shocked, saddened tone.

"Eric," she bawls.

"Eric?" Coach says. "You mean Weintraub? Well, I just saw him on the bleachers with the other boys. Looked pretty alive to me."

Melissa wails.

Eden goes over to Coach and whispers loudly in her ear. "It's a code blue."

Coach frowns. "Blue? Y'all set up a code blue." She rolls her eyes. "Now, what is that?"

"Uh . . . you know, blue, for sad."

"Sad. I can see that. But why?"

Eden looks at Melissa and frowns that she's sorry. "Blue for . . . boys," she says. Eden sinks to the bench with Melissa.

Coach puts her hands on her hips. "Sanchez, get a tissue and dry those eyes. I don't do code blue, so neither does this gym class. To the bleachers, ladies."

"I'm sorry your kiss was bad," I whisper to Melissa in the hallway to the gym. But at least she got one.

"Gloria Jean!" Eden hisses.

"What?"

"It wasn't her kiss that was bad!"

"Huh?"

Eden sighs. "It was *his* kiss that was bad. She didn't do anything wrong."

"Well, neither did I, and Connor still didn't try." I start speed walking away from them.

Melissa sniffles and pulls on my shirt to slow me down. "Connor didn't kiss you?"

I shake my head.

"At least you didn't choke."

"True, but I was sick in the bathroom for a little while."

That shocks Melissa's tears and snot dry. "Oh wow, that theater must be cursed or something! Did he at least text you this weekend?"

I shake my head. I want to run back to the locker room so I can cry, but I don't want Coach Nuñez thinking that it's my usual run for what she now calls code brown. I wish we'd never come up with the coding system, even as a joke, during her Lady Boot Camp seminar at the beginning of the year.

"Oh, Glorie Jeanie, you didn't tell me that." Eden rubs my shoulder. "I'm sorry I didn't wait for you."

Melissa links her arm in mine. "Boys who kiss bad are just bad." She squeezes my hand, and I squeeze back.

Once we climb onto the bleachers, Coach Nuñez stands in front of us girls. Coach Michaels stands in front of the boys.

"All right, listen up," Coach Nuñez says. "Starting today, the first Monday of every month we're going to have a special seminar on various topics related to sex education."

Several of the boys snicker. Eden raises her eyebrows and nudges me. Melissa puts her hands in her face. I know what she's thinking. Forget sex, can we please just be taught how to get a boy to kiss us properly? Olivia, the only girl to not use the shirt shimmy move, manages to look both bored and amused at the same time.

Coach Michaels reads from a paper. "Sex education is a continuing education. You can't learn it all in one class. The sex education program will help you to have healthy bodies and make healthy choices."

More whispering. Coach Michaels's usually deep voice is getting thin, and not because he's quietly angry, which he was once when Eric was goofing around with a pair of basketballs. Coach Nuñez rolls her eyes. She takes the paper from his hand and whips it in the air.

"Attention! The school board has determined that you are capable of learning this material as responsible students, so I expect you all to be mature about it. There will be no talking, no snickering, no joking around. If you heard something about this class from previous students, then you have not heard anything. That was their class. And now this is my class. This is Coach Michaels's class. There have been changes. Just clear your minds."

I have not actually asked any previous students anything about this class. J.P. had the first version. It's not exactly something you talk about at the dinner table. He tried, but then the following weekend Dad took him fishing at Lake Okechobee, and afterward J.P. and I didn't goof around as much as we used to. I don't know if that was because of the weekend or because he was fourteen and I was just nine. Eden's sister, Sarai, had this class two years ago, but she acts a lot like she wants nothing to do with us, which is weird 'cause just two summers ago she was letting us play with her makeup. Now she yells when we try to borrow clothes from her closet for when Eden wants to meet Zack at the mall or the movies.

"We are starting off with introductory material this week," Coach Michaels says haltingly. "An orientation. Each month from here on out, the subject matter will get more in depth and technical. This year we *are* allowed to answer questions."

Eden's hand shoots up in the air. "My sister said that she and the other girls were split up into different rooms from the boys. Are we gonna do that, too?"

Please oh please oh please, say yes. Melissa and I look over at the boys on the far side of the bleachers. Some are elbowing Eric and Connor and making kissing faces at us. Great. I bet one of the guys was at the theater and put the whole thing on the Internet. Ugh. Even though middle school is the time we can finally use social media with minimal parental control, it is also exactly the worst time to be so social.

"No," Coach Nuñez says. "You'll all be learning this together."

"Kyle, ATTENTION!" Coach Nuñez barks.

They clench their mouths shut.

"Coach Michaels, if you'll just get your packet, you can start on page three."

Coach Michaels snatches the booklet off the floor and begins to drone on. Coach Nuñez stands with her feet hips width apart, arms folded across her chest. Her eyes do this sweeping glare, like a lighthouse beam, across the bleachers.

Coach Michaels sounds like one of those adults in cartoons. In between the garbled "wah-wah-wah," there's stuff about maturity and hormones and changing bodies. Mom already had The Talk with me right before sixth grade. In the car, which is the worst place to have it. So while there's no seatbelt trapping me here in the gym, I'd really like to use a legitimate code excuse to go back to the locker room. But how can I let Coach know without announcing it to the whole gym or to the boys? I can't.

For the rest of the hour, I absentmindedly scratch my back and stare at the basketball hoop so it looks like I'm paying attention to Coach Michaels, but really, I'm thinking about the jar of oats sitting in the bathtub. My Poppa gets bad rashes, too, so when she was alive, Gigi used to draw him baths, as she called it, and she'd sprinkle oats in. Right before she died, when I was in the third grade, I had the chicken pox, and she stayed home with me, and drew me baths and told me the oats would make my skin feel better. She put them in tiny jars with ribbons on the lid so I could say they were some fancy European bath salts, if I wanted to impress my friends. But friends don't talk about the bathroom.

Eden flicks me with a paper, and I realize where I am. "What?"

It's a permission slip. A long list of subjects sits in the middle. I only recognize a few of the words.

"Settle, settle," Coach Michaels says. "There are many issues regarding sex. If you choose to have it. You don't have to. This form tells your parents what topics we'll be covering in class. We'll need their signatures turned in before you can attend next month's seminar. They can mail it in if you're too embarrassed. But there's no need to be embarrassed if your parents won't sign. It's a family decision. Those students not attending seminar will have alternate health studies in the library."

The bell rings. Eden, Melissa, and I jump up quickly and scan the forms. We've got five minutes to get our bags from the locker room and get to the next class.

"Why do we have to show this to our parents?" Eden jabs the paper with her thumb near the letters STI.

Melissa shrugs. "What's gon-or-*rhe*-a? Oh man, is it like . . ."

I shudder. The last thing I need is for anyone to confuse my runs to the bathroom with anything related to this class.

And then Olivia Calamatto walks by. Of course. And she's heard. The. Whole. Thing. "No. Don't be stupid."

"And how would you know?" Eden asks. Her hands are on her hips.

Olivia shakes her long hair and cocks her head. Her voice is womanly. I think that comes from the fact she had to go to pre-first grade after kindergarten, so she'll be turning fifteen at the end of the year. "My older sister had this class four years ago. Some guy came to class once and just talked about how abstinence is the only way to protect against the dangers of sex."

"Sex is dangerous?" That was not part of the Talk. Eden and Melissa look confused, too.

Olivia laughs. "Oh, aren't you two cute. Swallowing Sanchez. And Gloria Jean, Virgin Queen. Heard Connor wouldn't seal the deal." She smirks.

Eden crumples her paper in her fist. Melissa looks like she's swallowed the gum all on her own. My insides are twisting. Why does Olivia have to know *everything*? Does she honestly think she's better than us just because she's so much more developed and knows about guys?

"Connor . . . is . . . a gentleman," I manage to choke out.

"That's right!" Eden says.

"And it was just gum!" Melissa practically shrieks.

Olivia snorts. "Sure, honey, this time." She swishes her long honey-colored, curly hair around her other shoulder. "Better hope your parents sign those forms. Looks like you've got a lot of learning to do."

I bang my back against the locker, which cools the burning on my back. What did Olivia mean by "this time?" What could be worse than gum?

"I gotta go to the nurse." I heave to Eden.

"Just because of what Olivia said? Don't listen to her. You're smart. I'm smart. Melissa's smart. If anyone's got learning to do, it's Olivia."

"Yeah!" Melissa says. "Too bad there isn't a how-to-be-a-nice-person class."

Eden stuffs her crumpled form into her backpack.

I rub my back. "Thanks. But no, it's . . ."

"Oh. Right. Sorry."

I'm too queasy to correct her. I let my backpack hang off one shoulder as I zoom through the halls to the front office.

6

Nurse Robben sits at her small little desk. Her glasses are perched halfway down her long, thin nose. "Gloria Jean! The blue or the pink?"

"Green!" I gasp.

She looks at me funny. Usually I get a certain colored medicine depending on what problem I have.

"Aloe," I say and raise my shirt to show her the rash.

"Ouch. That is a bad one. Spend too long at the pool?"

I shake my head. "No, it's not a burn. It just happened this morning."

She grabs a bottle from a cabinet and squirts a big glob of the green goo into my hand. I start rubbing it in. I finally exhale in relief.

"Oh, did you eat something you don't usually have that maybe you were allergic to? Sometimes skin breaks out because of that. But this doesn't look like hives."

"Just some homemade bread last night. My Gigi's recipe. But I've eaten it before, when I was little."

"Hmmmph. Well, the aloe should help with the pain and itching. If that doesn't clear up, I say you go see a doctor. And I've been saying that a lot lately, Gloria Jean."

I flop onto the cot and speak into the paper covering. "Yeah, I know. Can I stay here until it's dry? Please? This is a new shirt."

Nurse Robben starts fussing at her desk. "It is very pretty. I like that coral color on you. It would be a shame to get all that goo on it." She kneels down next to me and gently turns my head toward hers. "But I think that goo will be dry in fifteen minutes, you hear?"

I nod and the paper crinkles.

"Okay. I'm going to step outside for a bit. On my desk, there's the release form your parents have to re-sign so I can keep helping you out. And with that, there's a note that I want them to read, okay?"

The paper crinkles again. "Okay," I whisper.

I hear the door softly shut. I reach up for the note. Great. Another written permission thing. And a warning.

Melissa and I are wrong. Boys aren't bad. Bodies are bad. I mean, swallowing gum when you're kissing is awful enough. Gum stays in your stomach for seven years. As if I of all people need that!

I decide that on the way out, I'm going to toss Nurse Robben's note. She and the coaches are just making it harder with their consent forms and warnings. But it's my body and I'm gonna make the rules.

* * *

For the next two Thursdays, Mom makes a puppy dog pouty face every time she's early to pick me up from Confirmation class.

"Still haven't connected with any of the kids in your class?"

"Nope."

"Well, that's a shame."

"Mom, they're all in seventh grade."

"So?"

"So? So, it's weird! I should be getting confirmed *this* year. It's like I was held back."

"Is that why you're not so chatty about religious ed this year? You're angry we delayed the classes a year?"

I kick my ballet flat shoes off and prop my feet on the dashboard.

Mom clicks her tongue, but I don't put them down.

"Well, I'm sorry. But last year you were constantly coming down with something . . ."

"Yes, I know, I was such a *problem* child and I was deliberately causing the Troubles."

Mom's voice gets louder and tighter. "And you were in the hospital during the whole weekend of the mandatory retreat with what the doctors thought was a horrendous stomach virus . . ." She's about to cry.

I fold my arms and shift uncomfortably in the seat, trying not to remember the pain, the mess, the smell, the fear that I had somehow come down with the world's youngest case of digestive cancer. We do have family history—Poppa is in treatment for stage one intestinal cancer. Luckily, it wasn't that for me. Just months marked by random phases of malnutrition, anemia, hours upon hours being "indisposed" or gas during Mass or class, and even once symptoms that suggested scurvy, which we learned in Social Studies was a disease pirates got when they didn't get enough Vitamin C. Dr. Yam put me on these ginormous-sized vitamins and I got better. But the Troubles came back. They always do.

"You didn't hold me back in school," I grumble.

Mom takes a deep breath, turns down the radio, and looks at me. "It's not your fault. Don't ever think we're blaming you. We will figure this out, I promise. School-work you could make up. But your father and I agreed that you can't really 'make up' getting the whole picture of your faith. Learning how it fits into your life and helps you make decisions is just as important as letting your body heal."

With that she looks away. The light turns green, and that's the signal for Mom to change the subject. "What's new with Eden and Melissa? And Zack and that Eric boy and Connor?" She says the last part really fast and nudges me on the arm. "Decided boy-girl parties aren't really for you yet?" She smiles.

"It's fine; whatever." If she thinks letting me prop my feet up and mentioning my actual-grade friends means everything's okay, she's wrong.

"All right."

"Where are we going? Home's left."

"I thought I'd take us to a dessert bar and we'd have some girl chat. I'll let you have coffee," she says in a sing-song voice.

Oh no oh no oh no. But not to the coffee. To the chat. "About what?" I try to say this like I'm five and sweetly curious. I want to be nice. I mean, it is free cake, and the good kind, not the dry stuff we eat at the nursing home whenever we visit Poppa.

"Well, you're getting to be that age. You're spending time with boys unsupervised and you and your friends watch that show about dating and all, I feel it's time we had a talk."

"We already had The Talk! Two years ago! In this very car. That," I point to the dashboard, "is where I spit out my soda."

"Yes, but see, The Talk is more like a process; it's ongoing."

I sink lower into the seat. She sounds like Coach Michaels's pamphlet.

Mom's mouth keeps going. "So, I thought we'd start having a girls' night, just the two of us. Your father can have his poker night. And I wanted to do it after your Confirmation class, because as with anything, especially 'ess-ee-ex,' God should be part of the equation. You know the er, physical operation, but I want you to know the spiritual relation."

Mom is *very* lucky I am not drinking a soda. I almost wish I was. Or a latte. Or grape juice, just so I can make a big ole splatter all over the windshield. "But . . . but . . . but . . . WHY?"

"Why? Gloria Jean, sex is sacred, for a man and woman who are married."

"No, no, I mean why do we have to go talk about this at the dessert place?"

"I told you, your father is starting a poker night. You know, we grown-ups like to do things with our friends, too."

She is not getting it at all.

"But I don't want to talk about that stuff in public!"

Mom slowly nods. "It's nothing to be ashamed or embarrassed about, sweetie."

I throw my hands up and look at the rearview mirror to see if the Coach Michaels pamphlet is there and Mom is reading from it word for word.

"Yes it is!"

Mom sets her jaw. "Okay, how's this? We'll start slow. Goodness knows I don't want to jump into the deep end, myself. You're still my little girl." She strokes my cheek and then puts on the windshield wipers. "Why don't you tell me what you learned in class today?"

I stare at the light mist outside the car. "G.E. Lights Never Die."

"What, dear?"

"G.E. Lights Never Die. GELND. The first five books of the Old Testament."

"Ohhh . . . how clever. So you can remember. Did you just learn the names or did you read anything? What was your favorite part?"

"Ehh . . . just got the highlights. Like, Genesis is the creation story, not a band. Whatever that means. Mrs. Fermacelli sure thought it was funny. Um, Numbers is really just a bunch of names and numbers. Deuteronomy was about deliverance—Moses preaching sermons. Oh, and L-laws—Leviticus was a bunch of random laws."

"Oh, and what did you think of the laws?"

"Some of them are kind of ridiculous."

"Like . . ."

"You know."

I know exactly what she wants to hear, and she's not going to get me to say it. There's a lot of weird rules about touching. Especially for girls during *that* time of the month. Back then, we couldn't even go outside because we were considered "unclean" and it was always so obvious to everyone. Really embarrassing. I bet Mom could handle Leviticus times just fine because Mom's the kind of mom who likes to tell me the story of when she first became "unclean" and is anxious for me to tell her when I finally have that magic moment. She says if it hasn't happened by the new year, she'll add that to the list of talking points with Dr. Yam. Dad's way of handling it is to brightly ask if there's anything else I need on the grocery list, and I just shake my head, he nods, and the cart moves on. Like this conversation needs to.

Mom pulls into the parking lot. "Well, if you ever have any questions about that part, you know you can ask me, right?"

I nod. She's hit every bullet point on the Coach Michaels pamphlet.

"So what was your favorite part about Confirmation class?"

"Exodus. We saw clips from that movie, *The Prince of Egypt*, but I've seen that already with Eden. My favorite part is when the Red Sea splits apart, because as the people walk through, they're in awe of the sea all around them. But they also feel nervous because at any minute the waters could come gushing down, but when they did, the people were safe, and it was this huge wave of happiness." I don't tell her that that's what I hope my first kiss is like.

Mom harrumphs as she unbuckles her seatbelt. "So this is what you're learning? How you're learning the faith? I would've thought Mrs. Fermacelli would've been more . . . by the book."

I nudge her elbow with mine. "Well, that'd be Miss Tompkins, the co-teacher. She makes sure we go through a lesson in the actual book."

"Still. I guess I'm just surprised. With bringing back the Latin Mass, I'd expect a class like that wouldn't be our parish's style."

"Hey, I'm learning, right? And I actually like it!" I put a little squee into my voice.

She lets her seat belt whap against the window as she unbuckles. "Let's go in, hon. We'll put this conversation on hold for now. I need some cake."

"Wait!" I pull out a tinted lip balm Eden got for me. I slather it on and smack my lips real loud and make a kissing face at the mirror.

"Honestly, Gloria Jean," Mom says, shaking her head. She leaves the car.

"What?" I hastily grab my backpack. Seriously, what? A rare October cold front has come, which, in Florida means it's only sixty-five degrees, but it's enough to chap my lips.

IV

Thou shalt
wear lip balm.

7

On Saturday, Eden comes over to plan our social studies term project. "Gloria Jean! Are these your designs for the contest?" Eden looks over each of my drawings.

My theme is Fall Flight, like flights of fantasy and the flight of curled up leaves as they float on cold winds. Florida does not have such a Fall, so it's kinda like a fantasy for me.

"They're just the initial plans." I shrug. "Still kind of rough."

"They're beautiful!" Eden beams at me. "I *love* the ruffles on this coat."

"Thanks. I hope it will stand out." I pick up a couple of the other papers and think about how I might make them even better.

Designing for Fall also means I don't have to worry too much about hem length and necklines. When we were all in the mall last month, we went to the sale racks first, and they had all the summer stuff on clearance. It got really hard for me to find something Mom would okay and something I would *feel* okay wearing. I tried on this one thing, and Eden's comment was "Girl, are you sure that's a skirt and not a belt?" Melissa laughed. "At least she's got the legs for it! I am so pale! This halter is showing all my tan lines." She went back into the fitting room. But I got this funny feeling in my stomach that I was pretty sure was not the Troubles. I threw one of my dress options over the door to her. "Maybe you should go more 50s. Retro is in." Melissa's eyes lighting up at the sleeves made the feeling go away.

"Ohmygoodness!" I sit straight up.

"What?"

"You know what we should totally do for the Gio project?"

"What?"

"The cultural history of clothes!"

Eden sits up straight. "Yeah! And our media part could be a video podcast. We could do a slideshow of outfits and talk about them. It would totally stand out."

"It definitely would. Great idea!"

Evidence #3 that Eden and I are meant to be best friends forever: we make a good team.

Eden runs her hand over my designs again. "Did you hear that Olivia entered the contest?"

I shake my head.

"Well, I think you've got it in the bag. I mean, what could she possibly design? Remember last year when we were on that science camping trip, and all her outfits were so skanky . . ." Eden sets down the drawings and then starts aimlessly thumbing through our social studies book.

I don't want to talk about Olivia, especially how the guys playing volleyball kept staring at her and didn't even look at us when we tried to hand them their ball back. But it transitions nicely into the next big piece of news. "My mom tried to have The Talk with me the other night." I tap my book with my pen.

Eden looks up. "Oh man. Again?! When? Where? How?"

"In the car. After my Confirmation class." I look down at my book.

"Oh man! *Why*?!" Eden nudges her book away with her foot and hugs her knees. When our moms gave us the Talk around the same time the summer after the fifth grade, we spent many sleepovers sharing the details.

"Yeah." I stretch across the floor. "Apparently this is a 'process' and we are going to be having a lot of conversations." I try to do an imitation of Coach Michaels. I fail.

Eden giggles anyway. "So what does your mom have to say about kissing?"

"Oh, we're nowhere near that yet. She started with what I learned in Confirmation class."

Eden leans forward. "Again, why?"

I pick at a nail. "I dunno. She says God is a part of it, so we have to talk about him first."

"Huh." Eden leans back onto my dresser.

"Yeah. I dunno. You think they're gonna talk about God at the sex ed thing in a couple of weeks?"

Eden shrugs. "I dunno. I overheard Olivia's sister telling Sarai this one time that they did at her class, but she could tell the people teaching didn't want to."

I pick at a thread of carpet. "Think they're going to start slow, and start with kissing, and then work their way up to sex, or just start with the big stuff?"

Eden lies on the floor and faces me. "I dunno. Parents and teachers always think we're all beyond kissing, anyway. And they always seem to want you to figure things out the hard way."

"Like with your first kiss." I smile at her.

"Yeah," she breathes. She turns onto her back and stares at the ceiling. I've heard her tell this story a million times, and as bad as it is, for some reason she loves to tell it again and again. "It was winter in New England, last year. I was visiting my cousins and we were going skiing. And I met this really cute guy, Mark, at the hot chocolate stand. We rode the lift all day. But it was snowing on and off and my lips were *so* rough and raw and flaky and gross. But he didn't care. Later that afternoon, when he dropped me off at the lodge, we stood outside, and it was snowing ever so lightly, and he stood there and I stood there, just looking at each other and then he came toward me and we kissed. It was soft and sweet and slightly to the side."

Romantic right? Everyone awws when they hear it. And by that point, that's how I wanted my first kiss to go, too. But I, and only I, get to hear the rest. I rest my head on my hands and stare at the ceiling, too.

"My lips felt so silky and smooth after, I just had to lick them. And that's when I tasted the blood. My lips had finally cracked. No matter what people tell you about kissing, they never tell you to start wearing lip gloss for like three weeks before you even think of kissing someone."

I peel myself off the floor and go to get my backpack. I want to put the balm on right now. "It's gone!"

Eden frowns. "Oh no! That was the really good kind, too, from The Beautique! Want me to help you find it?" She starts rummaging around my desk and finds the sex education permission slip, still blank. "You never showed this to your parents? So you're not going then?"

I didn't tell her about Nurse Robben handing me piece of paper after piece of paper. I have my reasons why I don't want to sign up. After the way she acted that Monday, I never thought Eden would actually want to sign up, either. Something in her voice just now makes me think that when she was trying to make me feel better, she was pulling a friend version of the Pajama Test. "You *want* to take the class?" I ask.

She flops onto my bed. "Okay, I know what I said earlier. But when I got home and Mom asked me how my day was, I realized we *have* to go. Think about it. It's either the class or more time in the car with our moms." Where my mom is slightly embarrassing because she treats me like

I'm still a kid, Ms. Abrams is embarrassing because she tries to talk and act like *she's* cool and young.

"Hmm. Good point."

"You don't have much time to mail it, unless you want to hand it in in person."

"That is not an option."

"Good. Get it signed right now. I'll look for your lip balm." She rolls off my bed.

"Okay."

Mom and Dad aren't home. I leave the paper on their nightstand.

8

It's Tuesday afternoon in Mr. Giopolous's social studies class. I'm sitting at my desk, racing to finish my multiple-choice test. The Troubles are hitting big time. I need to get to the nurse's office and get some medicine. *Bad*. I fill out the rest of my answer sheet and raise my hand. Mr. Giopolous comes over.

"Are you sure you're done, Gloria Jean? You have thirty minutes left, and if you hand it in now, I won't give it back."

"Yeah. I have to go to the bathroom. It's fine. I'm fine."

"Gloria Jean, are you sure?" he whispers. "I thought we were working on raising your average."

I'm starting to sweat. "I know. It's okay. I studied all day Saturday." Please please please please please, let me go.

"Alright, if you're sure."

I nod and then bolt. I feel like I'm in preschool and about to have what the teachers called an "accident." I absolutely do not want to have a most embarrassing moment ever, right here in the hall. I crash into the bathroom door and then yank it open. Good. All the stalls are empty.

I lock myself in the last stall. The physical wave of agony is soon over. But then another, different kind of wave crashes around me. That was close. So, *so* close. I do not want to go back to class, like somehow everyone will be able to tell. But I also don't think I can stick it out alone in here until after school lets out. I take my phone out of my pocket and scroll through my contacts to see who will feel the most sorry for me.

Mom said my cell phone was never to be used at school unless there was an emergency. I think this counts as an emergency. I am sick. I may be sick again in twenty minutes. I could call her or Dad, but then I'm afraid it'll remind them too much of last year. And the cancer word. And Poppa, who's always needing something at the home, and who wears diapers. Oh man, do I need to start wearing diapers now?

I would curl up on the floor, but this is the bathroom after all. Instead, I stand and cry. Big hiccupy sobs and I'm so glad I'm not in front of a mirror because I can just tell my face is all gnarled and ugly.

I am cold and I am panicking and crying like the little kid I feel I am. No boy will ever date me. I kick the tiny little trashcan in the stall. Then I get an idea.

I text Eden. Her phone's always on, just on silent. CODE RED!!!!! :D

Seven minutes later, she's in the bathroom, according to the plan we worked out ages ago.

She tosses over a change of jeans and whatnot from my gym locker. "Welcome to the Club, dearie Jeanie!"

Though there's nothing wrong with them, I scrunch out of my pants and into the jeans. If I'm gonna fake this, I should at least go all the way. "Did Gio give you a hard time?" I call out from the stall.

"Nope. Just told him I had to go to the bathroom. He did ask me to check on you, though."

"Oh no. Go back and tell him I'm fine. I'm not sick."

"Don't worry, I didn't say anything. Just winked."

"What?"

"Relax, GJ. It's middle school. They kind of expect it. Besides, I think Coach Nuñez gives 'em training about handling the womanly change with delicacy or something."

I snort. Okay, that worked for a second. "But still! I don't want him knowing. . . ."

I walk out of the stall with my actually clean, folded pants in hand and run into Eden's filing-nails attitude. "Fine, can you *whisper* to him when you go back that I just had to go to Nurse Robben and might as well go home from there?"

"Okay. You want to call your mom?"

"No. Why would I do that?"

"Glorie Jeanie, you're a woman now!" she gushes in a perfect imitation of Mom. "She'll probably buy you chocolate."

My stomach gurgles. "Uh, I'll be fine. Like the women in Sparta. Or was it Athens? Great. I got that question wrong on the test."

Eden just shakes her head. "See you later, *lady*." She winks.

I trudge to the nurse's office to wait out the rest of the period.

"Gloria Jean! How are we feeling today, my favorite chickadee?" Her face falls.

"Not good." I collapse onto the cot. One by one, the reasons flake off until my heart bleeds.

Nurse Robben just nods when I'm done. She gets up off her stool and goes to the phone. "Your parents never got the note I asked you to give to them, did they?"

I shake my head.

"Okay. I'm going to have to call your parents and tell them what happened today and recommend that they talk with your doctor about having a particular blood test done. We're all going to work together to make sure this doesn't happen again, okay?"

A week later, I sit in Dr. Yam's office and have my blood drawn. Turns out the note I gave Nurse Robben said that I should have the test for antigens again. Now, even if it comes back positive for just the one, they think they'll finally have an answer. A disease.

The cute lab technician, Mr. Vampire, smiles as he puts a neon purple bandage on my left arm. Three weeks ago, heck, three hours ago, I would have been wishing that I had put on some lip gloss because some handsome guy might be in the waiting room, see me, and want to kiss me and make it all better. It'd be soft and to the side and he'd have deep brown eyes.

Instead, the technician hands me a sheet that describes the latest disease the Troubles could be, with long paragraphs after bolded words. It looks like the handout we just got at Confirmation class that explains each line of the Nicene Creed, only that was in English, and this thing—with its tTG-IgA and EMA-IgA initials—looks like spy codes, only there's no decoder ring.

On the way home, Mom chatters on about how I should go to the Halloween dance on Friday. Are any of my friends from the movie night going? Maybe the party will be fun. Who is this Kyle Sneed she's heard mentioned? Is he new? And by the way, she forgot to tell me, but maybe thought I was too shy and didn't want it acknowledged, that she signed that form for the special seminars and mailed it in. Finally she turns around to look at me in the back seat.

"You just seemed so embarrassed in the car last time. But I do want you to have that information. Maybe you'll feel more comfortable learning it at school. But we'll check in. Especially after what Mrs. Fermacelli and Miss Tompkins have in store for you."

I get clued in to what Mom is talking about on Thursday. Apparently at the start of our Confirmation program, all the parents had a meeting with our priest, Fr. Mazi, the coordinator Mrs. Gomez, and Mrs. Fermacelli, and Miss Tompkins. They were told that part of our studies for the sacrament was going to be talking about "ess-ee-ex." No wonder Mom has the language down pat. She's been getting help with the lines from the beginning.

This week in class, we learn about Adam and Eve and how men and women are different —duh!—and how getting kicked out of the garden was punishment for Adam and Eve not following God's rules. I'm still not sure where the apple comes in.

Anyway, apparently, God designed us and our bodies in a specific way for specific purposes. Mrs. Fermacelli says it's called "theology of the body," meaning we can learn about God through our bodies. This sounds weird to me. She also teaches us another memory device: "Just think of the four *f*'s—free, faithful, fruitful, and forever." Miss Tompkins just sat smiling.

Both Mom and Dad pick me up from this class. Dad's sacrificed his poker night this week. Uh-oh. He's getting involved in The Talk.

We go to the same dessert bar. Mom and Dad look at me. I don't say anything, just swirl the cinnamon stick in my tea.

"Well, Gloria Jean," Mom starts.

Dad nods encouragingly.

"Relax! It's okay." Mom smiles a full-teeth grin that suggests maybe it's not. "You're coming into a special time of your life. This year you're getting a lot of information about how boys and girls and men and women interact.

And you may be interested in learning more about dating. That's normal. It's good you're coming to us, letting us know you're interested!"

Dad nods encouragingly. I'm trying to figure out how this is *me* coming to *them*. I am also trying to figure out how any of this is "normal."

"So we signed that form, and now we're going to let you hear two different ways to think about . . ." Mom swallows hard.

Dad nods encouragingly.

I stop twirling the stick. My eyes grow wide.

"Relationships." Mom quickly spoons some pie into her mouth.

Dad reaches into his pocket and pulls out a folded, slightly worn piece of paper. He slides it across the table to me, and nods encouragingly.

It begins with a quote from the priest our church was named after:

> Before [anyone else] speaks to them about life, you should speak to them—you and your husband. In the presence of God and with such tact, that they will hug you and say: Mom, how good you are. And how good Daddy is. How good God is for giving the two of you this power to bring us into the world. Do you see how beautiful this is? . . . The truth, at the right time, explained by mother or father. (Town meeting in Santiago, Chile on July 5, 1974)
>
> *Saint Josemaria Escriva*

I stop and look up. Mom has a hopeful smile. Dad nods encouragingly. So to them, The Talk is actually the

Truth. And while they may be letting me go to the class at school, I'm starting to see which side they're on.

"We know you learned about the four *f*'s today," Mom says.

I push back my chair and jostle the table. A bit of my tea splashes out. "Oh, come on! How do you even know that?"

"Gloria Jean! Would you RELAX?" Dad whisper-yells.

"Well, I'm never gonna relax if you keep telling me to relax like *that*."

"Like what?"

"Like there's a fire!"

He shakes his head.

I immediately sit back down.

"What is going on, dear?" Mom's knuckles are white from gripping her fork. It's like she's trying her hardest not to also whisper-yell.

"Why do you have to know everything?" It's just like Olivia being super-aware. Why couldn't what I was learning about private parts and what you could or shouldn't do with them remain, well, private?

"Because we're your parents," Dad says gently but firmly.

Mom mops up the splashed tea with one hand and signals to the waiter to get me another. "As I said before, there's a lot of information you'll be getting at both school and at church, and what you hear won't be the same. We trust you will come out of it able to know that real love is those four *f*'s: faithful, fruitful, free, and forever."

I chew on my cinnamon stick. "Okay."

"Okay." Mom quietly goes back to her pie.

Dad nods encouragingly.

On the way home, Mom lets me pick the radio station and I find my gloss in the car, wedged between the seat and the door, but neither makes me feel any better.

V

Thou shalt
keep your hands on
my face . . .
or belt loops.
I'm a good Catholic
girl, after all!

9

Zack and Eden are boyfriend-girlfriend officially.
They're wearing pieces of a couples' costume that I came
up with myself. There's this painting by a French artist of
a man in a hat and blue sport coat trying to kiss a girl in
a fluttery pink dress. Eden's still sporting the pink wrap
dress I found for her at a vintage shop, and Zack is wearing
only the hat and blue board shorts.

"Hot costume," New Kid Kyle says. He sidles up next
to me. I jump, and the cupcake I'm holding tumbles to the
stucco deck. Does he mean Eden's? I turn to see if she is
behind me.

"I mean yours. It's awesome."

He's right. My costume is awesome. I am wearing a pair of high-waisted brown pants, a silk scarf Gigi left me, a brown leather jacket I found at the consignment shop, and over-sized, bug-eye swimming goggles. Very retro, Eden had agreed. It's kinda the point. I wanted to look like Amelia Earhart, the famous pilot from like a hundred years ago.

"Thanks," I say. "I put it together myself. Looks like you could use a little help."

"Got any ideas?" he says in a rather low voice.

"Here. Goggles. Scarf. Now you're the Red Baron!" As I say each piece, I take mine off and put them on him. Look how bold I am! I want to find Eden and tell her how her rules for flirting aren't failing me yet.

He looks around at the party. We're pretty much alone on this part of the deck. "I still think I'm missing some-thing." His fingers scamper around my side and then glide along my belt. I jerk away, and my feet stumble along with me; it's hard to be graceful in tall brown boots.

"Ha ha. I need that, thank you." Seriously, these size zero pants from the juniors department are still too big, but there's no way I'm shopping in the girls' section (a.k.a. the adjustable waist section) in middle school, even if the smaller size pants fit better. Mom and I once got into an argument in the middle of the department store. She said if I was going to shop in the juniors section, then I needed to wear a belt; and I complained that I was the only girl still wearing belts with her jeans. "Yes, Gloria Jean," she had said. "A belt is a good way to keep your pants on. And not just from falling down, if you know what I mean." And I did then, sort of.

Now I know *really* well. I'd liked when Connor snaked his arm around me in the movies, but that was just around my shoulders! That's always been the universal sign that you were boyfriend-girlfriend. And according to Eden, it also leads to kissing. But an arm around the waist . . . what was New Kid Kyle after? The hot, tingly feeling is back on my neck, only it's now paired with a jittery leg. Whoa. Having a boy—a cute boy!—want to kiss me is a good thing, right? Then why do I feel so icky? Connor was taking it slow, like glacial, but this seems waaay too fast. Is that normal? I mean we haven't even been on a date! And we're not really dressed up! Did I bring this on myself when I flirted with him and gave him my accessories? I really don't like how he's trying to take more.

I pull off the boots and pretend to be really interested in the bubble stream's effect on my feet. No matter what I do, I feel like I can't cool off, and Kyle's making it worse. Why did I think "costume party at the pool house" really meant costume party, and didn't think to bring a bathing suit?

Kyle lightly nudges me. "Little shy, huh? You could always come over another time . . . just you and me . . ."

I hear a burst of laughter. Connor is bobbing nearby on an inner tube. He pushes off the wall with his feet and spins away toward the deep end.

Oh gosh. Is he laughing at me? At the idea of Kyle Sneed asking me out? How am I supposed to react to this? Seriously, why wasn't dating on the list of covered topics on the sex ed permission slip?

I can't make my mouth work to say anything.

"Playing hard to get, are we? I know that game. Don't let me win." Kyle hands back the goggles and scarf, chucks me on the arm then falls into the pool.

Melissa squick-flaps over to me. "Ohmygosh! What did Kyle want? What did he say? Are you interested in him?" Melissa toys with a limp, frizzy curl. "'Cause if you're not, I'd like, totally like to go out with him. Look at those lips! You know, he was held back a year."

Oh, do I know.

"He's probably had lots of experience. He'd know just how to handle gum."

Part of me wants to tell Melissa how creepy he is. But maybe Melissa likes that. She sighs dreamily.

"Or you know, you could just not chew gum." The glint of the sunlight on my eyes is as harsh as the tone of my voice.

"*Uch!*" Melissa crosses her arms and turns on her heels. She heads straight for the pseudo water polo match going on in the deep end.

I don't know why my lips can be so stitched up when it comes to kissing, but as open as the sky when I talk to people.

My stomach hurts. For once I can't tell if it's the Troubles or something else. Where is Eden? Last year, she always showed up when I needed her. It started in the summer, when I was always dehydrated. One Saturday she came over with a new swimsuit for me and we had a water balloon fight. I missed most of the first week of school because I was having really bad stomach pains. Since our favorite TV show at the time took place in England, Eden showed up with a white argyle sweater for me and we talked in British accents the whole afternoon. A month later, when I was out yet again, she claimed it was International Talk Like a Pirate Day, and brought me a fluffy white blouse and some ridiculously big gold hoop earrings and we spent the afternoon making corny jokes. Then, at Halloween, the Halloween we officially decided was our last not two weeks before, I was diagnosed as anemic, which meant I was tired and fainty and had an iron deficiency. So instead of trick-or-treating, she brought me Dracula fangs and a ruby-red lipstick. I told her "I vant to suck any blood but yours." Even though my body wasn't getting what it needed, I felt like I had all I really needed with my best friend there.

I find Eden swinging in a hammock with Zack. He's removed the hat and put on a hoodie. She's nuzzled up into the nook of Zack's arm. I go over to her. She doesn't see me, so I whisper into her ear. "Eden, I need to talk to you."

"Hmm?"

"I'm not having any fun. Any chance we can leave soon?"

"Have fun at the dance," she murmurs.

My heart plummets to my stomach. I go into the bathroom and call Mom. When she comes to get me, she of course has a five-minute chat with Mr. and Mrs. Sneed, who were occasionally looking out at the party from the living room. But even then, they couldn't see what was really going on.

Monday morning brings two things. The first is a call from Dr. Yam's office. We've reached the magic number of antigens, apparently. I need to have an endoscopy. It's this procedure where they stick a tube down your throat, into your stomach, and grab at your intestines. The appointment is Thursday. They're now certain that I most likely have this disease that's causing damage to my intestines.

The second thing is the big sex ed seminar. Great. Now I can learn how damaged I am in the boy department. As I walk into the gym, I see a clump of nine kids heading to the library. There are five girls and four boys. A couple of the girls I've seen at church before. I wonder why their parents didn't sign the forms.

I find Eden on the bleachers. She's sitting right in front of Melissa. Eden says "Hi! Don't you wish we could sit over at the other end with the boys?" Melissa just huffs and crosses her arms.

Coach Nuñez and Coach Michaels walk in with a woman wearing a *leetle* too much makeup and a prim skirt. "Atten-tion!" Nuñez announces. "This is Ms. Misty Parker. She's from the Healthy Communities group. The first lesson in sex education will be about making good choices."

"Thank you, Coach." Misty has a perky voice that makes her sound about four years old. "You all are coming into a special time of your lives. Your bodies are changing, and your feelings are changing. Suddenly, you find yourself thinking about acting in different ways without understanding why. And that is OH-KAY."

Is that what's going on with me? Why I was rude to Melissa on Saturday?

"With these thoughts, you're discovering that things you do with your bodies can feel good."

So, no, I don't get to excuse my bad behavior with puberty.

Misty Parker continues. ". . . kissing. Or touching. Or having sex. Each one of these actions is a choice. These things are only OH-KAY if both you and your partner agree to do them. If one person says no, you cannot do those actions. And it's perfectly OH-KAY to say no, to anything, as long as you want. Till marriage even."

Kyle laughs. "Some people don't even kiss till they get married? What freaks."

Eric, who is sitting next to him, smiles and nods like a bobble-head doll.

Misty laser beams her eyes onto Kyle. "Sit up, please. Then you'll hear me better when I say that questions should be reserved until the end of class. Now, let's look at the kind of information you need to have when making these choices. Can I have some volunteers?" No response. "No one? How about you, Mr. Freak?"

Kyle bounces up, takes a lollipop stick out of his mouth and cracks a big grin. "Yes, ma'am."

Olivia volunteers. Melissa starts down the bleachers almost immediately after. What is *that* about? Is she trying to impress Olivia? Connor sits on his hands. I do, too. Finally, Eric starts down the steps. He stands next to Melissa.

Misty pulls out a pizza box. "Let's say that this box represents some kind of sexual activity, and these volunteers each agree to engage in it." She gives the box to Kyle first. "Now pass it on!" Still sporting his cocky grin, Kyle hands the box to Melissa, whose cheeks are bright red. Eric glares at Kyle. Misty wiggles her forefinger at Melissa. "Keep passing, young lady." Melissa lightly chucks the box into Eric's hands. His cheeks are bright red, too. Olivia taps her foot. Eric holds out the box to her like he's presenting a queen with an offering. Olivia rolls her eyes and takes the box. She sets it at her feet. "No, dear, pick it up." Misty gives a fake adult smile. "For the exercise." Olivia sighs hard and picks it up. "Now open the box."

Inside are the letters STI. I wonder if that black spot on the inside lid of the box is a mushroom still stuck.

I wonder if anyone else in the gym is thinking the same thing. I wonder what an STI is. At least I've heard of STDs. Are they the same? All the initials I've seen lately float around my head like alphabet soup.

"What does this tell us?"

"That Melissa's a slut!" someone shouts from the boys' section. Giggles erupt. Coach Nuñez strides over and glares. That word is forbidden in her gym, and everyone knows it. Misty wrings her hands.

"Nooooo. That was a rhetorical question. I didn't finish. Your responses can come later."

Misty said as long as both people agree to sex, that it was OH-KAY . But if I want to kiss Connor and then later I wanted to kiss Kyle, if he were nicer that is, is that what guys would think of me?

Misty breathes in deep and looks heavenward. "No participation at this time. This exercise shows us that if we engage in sexual activity, we put ourselves at risk for an STI—a sexually transmitted infection."

Ohhh. But then what makes an infection different from a disease? Is it better or worse? When I was little and got a scrape, Mom always made sure it got clean so it didn't get infected. So it seems like an infection is something that doesn't have to happen, but a disease is something you have. It definitely sounds worse.

"If you do choose to have sex—and yes, oral counts— you must protect not only yourselves but also your partners *and* future partners."

"Yeah, no glove, no love!" It's another guy. Coach Michaels takes quick steps into the bleachers and stands among the boys.

"That's . . . right." Misty sounds tired. She walks over to her prop box and half-heartedly pulls out a pair of gloves and limply offers them to Kyle. He puts them on with gusto, making sure they snap at the wrists. "Ready!" He smiles with all his teeth at the girls' section of the bleachers.

Eden's eyebrows are about to jump off her face with alarm. My hand meets my forehead. Olivia finally throws down the box and storms off toward the locker rooms. Coach Nuñez runs her hand across her neck. She then walks over and directs Olivia back to the bleachers. She sits in a huff with her back to me. Melissa rushes over to the nearest bleacher bench a few feet away; Eric looks from Kyle to Melissa, and then back to Kyle again; and Kyle saunters over to the box, slowly pulls off the glove, looks straight at me. And. Winks. I want to run from the room, but cannot. Misty Parker, however, does.

Coach Nuñez faces the bleachers. "That demonstration illustrated three points," she barks. "One: When you 'hook up' as some of you call it, you are in a sense 'hooking up' with whatever diseases your partner had before you. Two: It is true that sometimes you will not know how many people your partner has been with. Mature, sexually active *adults*—"

"Which you are not," Coach Michaels says loudly.

"—thank you. Adults have open, honest conversations *before* getting into bed with each other."

I look down the bleachers. Olivia is resting her head on her knees, staring at the wall, away from the boys.

"Three: It is wildly inappropriate to broadcast any 'action' you have gotten. Gentlemen and ladies are

discreet. Now, because the state mandates you know
the material on the handout, please take one and pass it
along and read *silently*."

Eden pokes Melissa in the back. "Hey," Eden whispers.
"My older sister says hooking up can mean making out,
too. Not just doing everything. Do you think we can get
these diseases from that?"

Why is Eden asking Melissa and not me? Is it because
I've never been kissed? I can at least try to make her feel
better. "Oh, Eden." I give her shoulder a little squeeze. "It
says here it's only likely if he's done certain . . . other . . .
things with someone else. But Zack would never do that to
you." She and Zack really like kissing each other.

"What makes you so sure Kyle wouldn't?" Melissa
snarks. "Then again, maybe it doesn't matter to you.
He's all eager to use protection," Melissa says. She turns
around so her back faces me.

"Okay, you know what? Stop it," I say. "Yes, he talked
to me at the party, but he was coming on really strong. It
freaked me out."

Melissa turns around. "You're just saying that." She
puts her head in her hands.

"Are you sure?" Eden asks me. "He was just being a
stupid boy, joking around. He's really hot, but that doesn't
necessarily mean that he's so . . . so . . . experienced. He
invited all of us to his party. That was nice. Are you sure it
wasn't just normal flirting? Maybe all he wants is to kiss a
little bit."

"It's not that! I know. I mean . . ."

"Are you sure you're not just afraid? I know I was

scared at first when Mark went to kiss me. And maybe you weren't ready for Connor. You'll grow more comfortable. You heard what Misty said . . ."

I'm about to have a code green. Not as like green with envy like I learned in English class. As in the color my face is.

"I am *not* scared. And who do you think *you* are, Ms. Experienced? I was having *issues* at the movie with Connor."

"Maybe it's psychosomatic." Eden sounds like her mom that one time we overheard her therapy session with a client in her home office.

I grit my teeth, grab my backpack, and rush down to Coach Nuñez. I whisper to her. She nods. Inside the locker room, I sit on the bench and jiggle my leg. Best friends do not call each other psychos. I close my eyes, which intensifies the stinging behind them as I cry. I feel the bench shift under the weight of someone else. Fingernails dance on the metal.

"Um . . ." It's Olivia. "I know we're not, like friends or anything, but that wasn't cool. 'Cuz you're right. Kyle's got this player vibe. He's not for you."

"Then why do you want him so bad?"

"He's really hot. And pays attention to me." She says this last part as a whisper.

I wipe away the last tears with the back of my hand and look at her. She won't face me. She's not smiling.

"Thanks," I whisper.

I don't see Eden again until lunch. I almost don't want to sit next to her. But her eyes look hopeful as she waves me over to our usual table. I plop down on the bench. She pulls out her phone and starts to read: "Psychosomatic (adjective): having real, physical symptoms caused by thoughts or emotions. Synonym: can't think of any. Antonym: psychos."

Before I can say something, she holds up her hand and types something else into her phone.

"Psycho (noun): crazy person. Synonym: boy who doesn't think G.J. is awesome. Antonym: G.J.." She gives me a big smile and nods encouragingly. I crumple my brown lunch bag and get up. She has the psychosomatic reaction of crumpling her face.

"I've been having bad stomach stuff a lot lately," I tell her. "The doctor thinks I have a disease. Not an infection that can be cleared up with some cream or pill, and it's not someone else's fault. So now I found out that I have to go get some procedure done on Thursday, and I won't be in school. But you would have known a lot of this if you had been my real best friend and talked to me instead of making out with Zack all weekend. By the way, that doesn't make you better or smarter or more qualified to give lessons in kissing."

None of the girls at the table say anything. I spend the rest of lunchtime eating at the table nearest the lunch line. It smells like industrial strength cleaner and broccoli.

The rest of the week I can tell Eden's offended because I end up sitting at the edge of the smelly table and my usual spot is taken by Zack.

11

The morning of my endoscopy, I am freaking out because

1. I am not allowed to wear my favorite black yoga pants and T-shirt that has a palette saying "I am full of color!" Mom insists I wear my church skirt and a cardigan because *it's the doctor's office*, even though I will end up having to wear one of those awful paper gowns while the black rubber tube snakes all around my insides.

2. I have not been allowed to eat since last night's early dinner, in preparation for the black tube they're going to wiggle down my throat.

3. My mom has called the school and told them *exactly* what I will be doing and why. So now all my teachers know that my intestines are having issues, and they're very concerned about what this black snake thing will find. I hope they don't make a card for me.

and

4. Dad is worried about my gag reflex and says they'll have to put me under. Good. Did I mention I'm basically swallowing a black snake for an hour?

Dad's taken the morning off of work, and Mom switched around her shifts this week at the library so she can be with me all day. We drive to the hospital. I put on the paper gown that doesn't really close and get onto a bed. Right before I close my eyes, I think the nurse kind of looks like Nurse Robben.

When I wake up, Dad ruffles my hair. "Morning, sleepy bean." I'm still in the hospital bed. I must have slept through the whole procedure. Dad kisses me on the forehead and says he has to go to work. When I'm feeling awake enough to walk, Mom takes me home. At least I get to eat lunch in my yoga pants and shirt. She sits with me as I slowly work on a pile of mashed potatoes.

"The new specialist, Dr. Schmidt, says you should be back to normal by tonight." She says this in a sing-song voice and her eyebrows dance a little.

"You mean I still have to go to Confirmation class?" I worry down some potatoes. Sometimes we start the class by saying how our week was or something special we did. Let's review mine: the sex ed demo made everyone act weird—so weird that my best friend and I aren't talking—

and I just had a tube stuck down my intestines to check for celiac disease, which Dr. Schmidt joked was the trendy new thing. As if being diseased was the *it* fashion every girl should have.

Mom busies herself with the dishes. "Mrs. Fermacelli said it would be a good class, and the last one before your retreat and then Thanksgiving."

"Okay. Whatever." Maybe if Mrs. Fermacelli is taking the lead, it won't be so bad. I spend the afternoon thinking of happier things to say about my week. My designs for the fashion contest are looking pretty good. I'll say that.

Confirmation class is held in one of the small rooms in the multi-purpose building attached to St. Josemaria Escriva.

When I go inside, Hanna and Hallie, the twins, give me a small wave. Paul, their brother just a year older, doesn't really look at girls. Okay, so there's one person my age. But he's a little unapproachable. At our first class, when we went around the room saying who we were and one thing about our Catholic faith, he said he already knows what he wants to be when he grows up—a priest. Mary Bridget helps Mrs. Fermacelli set up speakers. I haven't really learned the others' names, so I've given them my own. There's Ms. Catholic Jeopardy, Shy Guy, Mr. I-Went-to-Rome-and-all-I-got-was-this-superiority-complex, and Nervous Tic. He has this habit of running his hands along his pants legs.

I take my usual seat on the floor with my back against the couch. Miss Tompkins leads us in a quick opening prayer. Mrs. Fermacelli stays by the radio. "Settle. Settle."

Everyone takes a seat in a semi-circle. "A few classes ago, I mentioned some things about the Theology of the Body. Part of living out our faith involves chastity."

My brow furrows. Huh? I mean, I've heard of "chastity belts," once in a movie. But that was set in the middle ages. Does that have anything to do with the music?

Mrs. Fermacelli clasps her hands. "A lot of people don't really understand what chastity is, or why it's important. So today, we'll look at chastity and talk about how it relates to love."

Okay, so clearly not about the music. I quickly sneak looks at the boys in the circle every time she says "chastity." I'm betting if Coach Michaels said that word, the boys, especially Kyle and Eric, would be snickering. But no one here is.

"You love your families and your friends, but what does it mean to say you love another person in a romantic way? God has a plan for what that should look like." Mrs. Fermacelli starts fiddling with her mp3 player. "To spark the discussion, we're going to listen to two very different songs."

A couple of the guys exchange looks. We girls perk up. Although, I wonder what kind of music Mrs. Fermacelli thinks really "speaks" to us. I know Eden's mom loves to blast the bubbly pop we listen to when she drives Eden and me around, but my mom can't stand it.

A slow, soft, strumming guitar glides into a husky guy's voice, whose first few verses are questions this guy has about a relationship. The last one is: "Can you kneel before the king and say 'I'm clean, I'm clean'?" I guess not, because the singer gets really angry. Clearly someone's been hurt by this really intense-sounding relationship. Toward the end, the tone changes, and the singer sounds a little hopeful when he begs twice: "Lead me to the truth and I will follow you with my whole life."

I lean back, hoping the guitar sounds linger.

Rome Complex is the first to speak. "Is kissing 'clean'?"

Now I'm sitting straight up. Ohmygosh. Are we the air-quotes "freaks" air-quotes that Kyle was talking about? Catholics can kiss, right?

Miss Tompkins furrows her brow. "Good question, Julian! What do you think? Is it *what* they did that matters to the singer?"

Paul raises his hand. "I don't think so. I think he was mad because he thought whatever they were doing meant they loved each other, but it really didn't because it didn't actually mean anything to the other person."

Mrs. Fermacelli's eyes grow wide. She smiles a genuine smile. "Exactly. The reasons *why* we do something make it clean or not. Sometimes kissing is a sign of love. And sometimes it can just be using a person to make yourself feel good. And that is not real love."

I chew on my lip. None of this was said at school. I try to make a mental list of the good, not selfish reasons why I want to go out with Connor and why I want a kiss. It's as blank as the chalkboard.

Mrs. Fermacelli takes a moment to look each of us in the eyes. "I know our faith has a lot of 'nos' that seem to go against our biology and hormones. But chastity is a way of saying 'yes' to the real love God wants you to both give and receive."

Mrs. Tompkins scrolls around on the mp3 player. A really beautiful slow song starts playing. "Your love is extravagant. Your friendship, it is intimate." I almost melt. You can tell he really loves whomever he's singing to. It sounds way deeper than the kind of love I hear about at school when so-and-so says she loves you-know-who. I close my eyes and pretend it's me. "Spread wide in the arms."

I think about Connor's arms stretching across the pool as he's about to dive into the deep end of New Kid Kyle's pool.

" . . . is the love that covers . . ."

I think about how he ends up in a belly flop, his body covering the water and sending it splashing over me.

"No greater love have I ever known. You considered me a friend. Capture my heart again."

My heart is so captured by this song I for once am not thinking.

When the song is over, I slowly open my eyes. My cheeks are pink. The lyrics sound too deep to be about a girlfriend. The singer keeps using the word "friend," though, which I thought wasn't as deep as loving someone romantically. What kind of friend is he talking about? Eden's my closest friend. Even though Eden and I aren't the same religion, we tell each other secrets and feel comforted by each other. I can trust her with anything. Or I used to. Now I don't know. Connor and I are sort of friends, from the time we all were at science camp last year. But we are not "intimate." Does the singer mean we have to be friends first?

Tic asks sort of a similar question about what happens when you're not friends first and you get intimate anyway.

"Well, Nathan, how would that make you feel?" Mrs. Fermacelli asks.

"Confused," Shy Guy pipes up.

"That's right, Ian."

That *is* right. I look at him for an extra five seconds. He has hair the color of sand and a glint of gold in his eyes, like sun bouncing off the ocean. In just that one word, I hear something in his voice that feels just like the heat of the beach day I now find myself imagining.

Mrs. Fermacelli explains that "There is no love without sacrifice," which is a quote by this saint, Maximilian Kolbe, who died in the holocaust. She reminds us of that Gospel verse where Jesus says that the greatest love is to give up your life for your friends.

Now that my brain is working again, I realize I missed that part of the lyrics—the love was about God. And I try to imagine what that kind of sacrifice would look like now in the real world, the eighth grade—to give up something very important to me because I thought that might do someone good. I'm not sure it's even possible.

I'm surprised, because what I'm thinking sounds a lot like what Ms. Catholic Jeopardy is talking about now.

"Right, Angela!" Mrs. Fermacelli says. "If you're being chaste, you're giving up doing something just because it feels good or you want it, because you know it's not good—not just for yourself, but also not good for the other person. *That* is a way to truly love someone."

Miss Tompkins goes on to explain that everyone is supposed to live chastely, not just nuns, or teens or single adults. If we ever need help figuring out if what we want to do is in line with our faith, we should ask ourselves if it really means something, if it's faithful, fruitful, free, and forever.

It's silent for several long minutes. I think about Monday's sex ed seminar and how none of the adults would look at us. How the "L-word"—love—wasn't even mentioned. How they used words like "partner," which when I say it over and over again in my head sounds dry and like something in a lawyer's office. How if any one had asked themselves if whatever they had agreed to do with someone was real love, then maybe there would have never been the passing of the pizza STI.

The class at school was all about protecting just the body; but this is about protecting your body *and* your heart. And about how my feelings about something as simple as kissing matter. And not just the kiss itself, but whether there's meaning behind it. This chastity stuff doesn't sound too bad.

"Gloria?"

"Hm?"

Ian's pushed his desk near mine. "Mrs. Fermacelli wants us to come up with ways we show people we love them 'with our whole hearts' like the song says without having to 'make love.'"

"Oh! Okay. By the way my whole name is Gloria Jean. My grandma used to say it's Gloria Zh-ah-n, like it was French and I was Joan of Arc, but that sounded silly."

"I like just Gloria. It sounds lyrical. Music's kinda my thing." The slightest wave of pink spreads across his cheeks, like it's the Red Sea, but rushing together. Suddenly I'm shy.

"What have you got?" I look at the list.

Cook your mom dinner when she's tired.
I mentally add, *make your daughter mashed potatoes.*

Make your friend laugh when he's had a bad day.
I think, *bring your friend pants, no questions asked.*

Sit with your little sister when she's crying and
comfort her.

Olivia did that. Does that mean she loves me? But this
also must mean that you can't be the one that makes her
cry. What does it mean that Eden can show she loves me
one day and then hurt me the next?

Listen to every word she says and prove you paid
attention when you answer.

So we can be chaste in how we speak or don't speak to
each other. Kyle did not listen to me.

Respect her and don't use her for affection. It will
show her you care more for who she is than what she
can give you.

In other words, don't touch her belt before even asking
what her favorite color is.

"Wow. That's a good list."

He blushes a little. "The last one's more from what we
just talked about. So not original. But thanks, Gloria." His
voice is gentle and his eyes sincere.

Gloria. I like that. Then it hits me. I think I'm getting a
glimpse of what a true gentleman looks like. This view is
kind of nice, especially with what Ian does next. He starts
a conversation.

"I see you doodling on the paper during class some-times. What are you drawing?"

"It's designs for this competition. Top prize is six weeks at a design summer camp and one of your looks made and put on display at a clothes store. There's another contest for designing boats. The winner goes to a nearby engineer-ing camp and gets to ride on the main yacht at the Boat Parade."

"That's awesome. I wish they had something like that at Saint Ambrose."

St. Ambrose is an all-boys school.

"Aww. Do you like to draw?"

"Yes. Don't tell Julian, but I like to go to this art store on 39th Street." Ian winks.

I smile. "Secret's safe with me."

"Knew I could trust you, Gloria."

Gloria. I really like the sound of that. And he can trust me! I suddenly remember that homily after the not-date date with Connor. More than anything I want to be trusted, with small things first and then bigger ones. What I don't want: below the belt touching or even on the belt touch-ing. Hands on the face, boys. Or at your side. Or holding mine. What *do* you do with your hands when kissing? But most importantly, I don't want to feel like I did at the pool party with Kyle. Or even like I did with Connor, who had nothing to say about anything at all—like I was doing all the work. No, sitting with Ian with his way of saying my name. Feeling like *this*.

VI

Thou shalt not
eat bread for forty-five
minutes before.
Like with swimming.
You could get cramps.

12

It's official. The Troubles are definitely celiac disease. On Monday afternoon, Mom and Dad go with me to the specialist, Dr. Schmidt. I sit on the examining table with my arms crossed. It's cold in the office, and I don't want Dad sitting there against the wall or Mom rubbing my shoulders. I do want to hear why I have the Troubles and how I can stop them. I just don't want to hear Dr. Schmidt say I have to give up cookies and bread forever or else the Troubles will come back ten times as worse.

"But Dr. Yam said even if I had this celiac thing, I could probably still eat whatever I wanted before that appointment when you stuck that tube thing down my throat last week," I say.

"The endoscopy, yes," Dr. Schmidt says. "When you have celiac disease, gluten damages your small intestine. Think of chunks of gluten acting like bowling balls zooming down your intestine, flattening these tiny little things called cilia. The cilia's job is to grab nutrients and absorb them into your bloodstream. If they're not working, it's hard for you to get proper nutrition." He flips through papers on a clipboard. "It's likely the reason you had so many problems last year. When you stop eating gluten, the damage stops. Since we needed to make sure the gluten was what was really causing the damage, we let you eat the way you always do. Now that we know what it is for sure, you cannot have any more gluten. No more regular bread, most kinds of cookies, and when you're older, no beer. . . ."

"No beer!" Dad says. "Oh, String Bean." He chuckles.

Mom lightly swats at his shoulder. "Honestly, Stan." She puts on a concerned frown when she turns to Dr. Schmidt. "Do you have a list of what she can and cannot eat?"

"Yes." Dr. Schmidt pulls a piece of paper from a file folder on the clipboard and hands it to Mom. She starts murmuring the list of stuff. She's murmuring a lot. Terrific.

"Now, Gloria Jean," Dr. Schmidt continues, "in addition to food, you have to be careful of what you do. Some people have a very high sensitivity. They're so sensitive they can't go into a bread aisle in the supermarket without feeling woozy. We don't know your sensitivity level yet, so you'll have to be extra careful. Even everyday things that aren't food contain gluten. For example, envelopes. So no licking!"

Good. I don't do that anyway. Eden taught me the trick of wetting a sponge or paper towel or something.

"No using flavored lip glosses that don't list ingredients."

Lip gloss! I fumble in my purse for the special pumpkin spice gloss I just got last Saturday. Without Eden. I can't find it. Please God, let it be fine.

"No touching bread or gluten products and then touching your mouth without washing your hands first. Mara," he turns to my Mom, who perks up, like they're now fast friends. "I'm afraid this means going totally gluten-free with your cooking. Or if you and Stan would like to have your favorites sometimes, you may need to get Gloria Jean her own set of dishes and cookware." Dr. Schmidt turns to me and smiles. "Maybe something with flowers?"

Whoa. This is getting a little ridiculous. I try to grab the list from Mom so I know just how many gluteny things I have to stay away from, but she swats my hand away.

"And, this may sound silly, but I have seen other girls your age with allergies having problems. Maybe even no kissing if your date's just had those foods."

"No kissing!" I yell.

Mom stares in horror at the list. "No Communion!" she shrieks.

"What?" Mom and I both ask, looking at each other.

We both look at Dr. Schmidt.

"As I was telling Gloria Jean, certain behaviors can cause problems. Actions like kissing, or receiving any piece of communion bread, even if it's just a particle you take in drinking from the same cup at church, can expose you to gluten, and later in the day, you may feel really, really sick."

Mom staggers back into a chair. "But we're Catholic! How's she supposed to give up Communion?"

I bite my lips. But I'm fourteen and I've never been kissed! All these rules I've been making up are for boys—not me!

"This is a disaster!" Mom and I say aloud, at the same time.

Dr. Schmidt sets the clipboard down on the examining table. "I know this is a lot of information all at once. But lots of people live with celiac disease every day. They have beer, their own kind of beer, sure," he says, winking at Dad. "And I believe there are gluten-free wafers or crackers you can use for Communion," he says to Mom, who has risen and is clutching the paper close to her chest. "And they definitely kiss," he says to me, patting me on the shoulder. I stop pressing my lips together and let the blood flow back into them. "I'll give you all a moment to let this sink in. I'll be back in a few minutes, if you have any more questions."

Mom falls back into her chair. "Jesus, Mary, and Joseph," she exhales.

Dad harrumphs.

I lie back on the examining table and try to find designs in the popcorn ceiling. I can't make anything out.

99

* * *

The next day, in gym, the boys are playing flag football on the field while we girls run around the track circling it. I'm feeling pretty sluggish. I see Eden's ponytail bobbing up and down next to Melissa's thick, wavy hair frizzing up in the humidity. My breath goes in out in out. Tell. Not tell. Tell. Not tell. I can't think of a cute thing Eden would get me or what accent we could use for celiac disease. But maybe I'm not giving her enough credit.

"Hey, Eden!" I call.

She looks over her shoulder, shakes her head, and whispers something to Melissa. She looks over her shoulder, too. And then rolls her eyes.

Finally, Eden slows down. Melissa charges on ahead.

"What?" Eden won't make eye contact.

"I . . . so last week . . ."

"Yeah, let's talk about last week. I try to give you friendly advice, and what do you do? You turn on me and Zack and our relationship." Eden is now looking at me, but fiercely. Her whole face, her voice, everything is pinched. "You know what it is? I think you're jealous. Yeah. I'm doing something first and you can't deal anymore. So instead of trying to be there for me, you just yell at me in front of the whole cafeteria. You just have to face that we're on different levels now." She straightens her posture and then slightly raises one shoulder and an eyebrow.

Pressure builds behind my eyes. I pull long breaths, focusing on the hot air cycling inside me, to keep me from having a code blue. "That's not fair," I say in a small voice.

Her eyes are cold. "You're right, it's not. And you know what else isn't fair? That we're getting nowhere with our social studies project because you're caught up in this body drama. You look fine to me."

I clench my fists and exhale loudly. I have no idea why she's challenging me, why she's changed. "Why don't we get together Thursday? I don't have my class."

She juts her chin up in an air of superiority, but narrows her eyes, like she's suspicious. "Right. Your religion class. Maybe that's what's really going on. Instead of doing stuff with me, you're now hanging out with them. They're feeding you all this stuff about sin and going too far so now you're judging me."

"That's not it!" My voice is shrill from the anger and the garbled tears.

Out of nowhere, Coach Nuñez is marching toward us. "Abrams-Adams! Wisnewski! Why aren't you running?"

Eden shoots me a dirty look. "Whatever. Just FYI, I'm now in Melissa and Amber's group for social studies. I cleared it with Gio yesterday. While you were absent. *Again*. You're on your own for this project."

And she jogs away.

I lift up my feet, which feels like I've got cement in my sneakers, though the rest of me feels drained. I whisper to Coach Nuñez that I'm not feeling well, clutching my stomach, and she excuses me to the locker rooms with a small nod. I wipe tears from my face with the back of my hand.

On my way in, I pass by the boys, waiting for the next play to start . Kyle whistles. I gulp back a scream.

"No, not you," Eric snarks. "That girl is trouble," he says to Kyle, nudging him. Kyle laughs. "Yeah man."

Then I see Olivia jogging by. Everything about her bounces. Her shorts are riding up.

I look down at my gym uniform. It seems like it's just dripping off my drooped shoulders. Like I'm not a person, just an ugly, defective hanger.

I shuffle back inside. Sitting in the cold air conditioning of the locker room, I scrounge around my backpack for the lip gloss. I come across some sketches for my designs. Maybe if I won this contest, I could use the prize money to buy some more make-up. Maybe then someone would pay attention to me. And it wouldn't be because of any Troubles.

13

That Saturday, on top of everything, I have go to a Confirmation retreat. It's a requirement for all the kids in all the Confirmation classes in our diocese. Which means Connor Riley will be there. I may have labels on my lunch bag and a note from Mom regarding snacks, but at least I do not have a pimple on my lip. Still no sign of the lip gloss I lost. I can't tell if this is God answering my prayer, just in totally the wrong way, or not. It's not fine. I so want to look pretty. Ian will be there.

"How're you feeling?" Dad asks. Rather than just dropping me off, he's pulled into a parking spot at this hall that some men's religious group owns in our town of Sable Palms.

"Okay, I guess." I swallow and look out the window.

"Well, if you're not really, you can always call, and I'll come get you. Not that far of a drive this week." He smiles at me.

"I know."

"Have you told any of your friends from class? What about Eden?" His bushy eyebrows make question marks with the moles on his temples.

"No one. And she's not in this class. And they're not my friends." I make a big show of unclicking my seat belt.

Dad looks down at his hands. "Right. Well, you're not that different from everyone else. Besides, this thing runs in families." His brows even out. "We called J.P. last night, and he might have it. He'll get tested. Then maybe the String Bean won't stand alone." He pats my hand.

I jerk it away and run it through my hair. "Da-ad. Stop calling me String Bean. I was reading on this forum that it could be the celiac disease that made me so skinny. Now I'll probably get fat. You'll have to come up with a new dorky name." I yank my bag from the floor of the car. "Gotta go."

Dad reaches for me. "Gloria Jean, wait."

But I've already got the door open and one foot out. "I'll see you at four," I say tightly. I can't go in there about to cry.

Dad's moustache frowns. "Love you, Str- sweetie." His voice is low, but full.

"Bye," I whisper, and slightly slam the car door.

Inside the main hall, I see some people from my class. Hanna and Hallie wave me over to where they're sitting. Ian is out of the navy school uniform pants and crisp white shirt he normally wears to class. Now he's got on a dull-lime green polo shirt and blue jeans. It actually coordinates with my purple sweater and light gray skinny jeans—though on me the pants look like regular weight jeans. It's a color combo I'm using in my designs.

Mrs. Gomez, the person in charge of the retreat, sits at the table with the nametags. I give her the note from Mom explaining everything. Her eyes widen, she jumps up, and walks away. I pick out a bright pink marker to write my name with. Then, I see him. It has been almost two months since the not-date date when Connor Riley did not kiss me. Nearly a month since the Halloween party when he laughed at me. Since I've been eating right, for like a week, I am still the skinny String Bean. But Connor has grown the tiniest of muscles on his arms and legs. He walks over to me.

"Hey," he says.

"Hey," I say.

"Are you okay? I heard you were in the hospital, and then you weren't at school on Monday, either. Kinda like last year."

"Oh, that. Yeah, it's nothing. I'm fine."

"You don't have like, a disease or something?" Connor lowers his voice.

"What? Oh, man, no." As the words leave my lips, I decide that they are not lying. I am not lying. If I'm going to be different, I'm not going to be diseased. I'll just call it a new diet. Girls diet all the time, right? "It was nothing, really. I'm fine."

"Cool," he says.

"Yeah," I say. I can't believe he's asking about me. And that last year he noticed how I was missing school. After the pool party we haven't spoken a word to each other. I guess if he's being nice today, I can be nice, too. "Did you ever see that action movie? I think it's out now."

He starts to smile *that* smile. Oh no. Am I falling into like with Connor Riley again?

"Oh, that one. No, I haven't," he says. "You into that sort of thing?"

"Sure," I say. Then I lower my eyelids ever so slightly like Eden taught me.

"Maybe we should go sometime," he says.

"Maybe we should." I clap my hand over my mouth. Oh no. What if we go out and then I have to explain the waiting rule? I mean, I can just hear it now. "Aww . . . I'd love, LOVE to kiss you, but not right now. Can you wait? Like 45 minutes? I'll set a timer?"

Connor looks at me funny. Oh, right. I remove my hand slowly to reveal a smile. That'll show Eden.

Father Mazi, our priest, who must have volunteered to lead the retreat, breaks the moment. "Gloria Jean," he says. "Can we speak with you a moment?"

I lightly touch Connor's arm. "I'll be right back." I walk off to the side. "Yes?"

"Gloria Jean," Father Mazi says. "Mrs. Gomez just told me you have been diagnosed with celiac disease. How are you feeling?"

Let's see . . . I'm really feeling like I want everyone to stop asking me how I'm feeling, especially since they all look at me like I'm dying as they say it.

"Fine."

"Good to hear," he says. "Now, this note from your mother says you've brought your own Communion hosts for Mass later this afternoon?"

I reach into my backpack and pull out the box of wafers and the small metal carrying case I learned was called a pyx. "Yup. It was the first thing Mom went out and got after we left the doctor's office." She and Dad used the GPS to find church supply stores. I never knew Communion started out as wafers in a roll in a brown box, like fancy crackers.

Mrs. Gomez smiles like you would at a cute kitten. "That's great! If you don't mind, I'll make sure they get on the altar with the rest." She looks at the list of the ingredients on the box. "Father? I've never seen this kind before."

Father Mazi peers over. "Uh-oh."

I look back at Connor and shrug, then look at Father Mazi. "What?"

"Where'd you say you got these?"

"I don't know. Some specialty store. They're made with rice, so I can have them."

Mrs. Gomez now frowns as if I'm a dying kitten.

Father Mazi hands me the bag. "I'm sorry, Gloria Jean, but we can't use these. For true Catholic Eucharist, the hosts must contain wheat."

"But!"

"I'm sorry. Truly, I am. I know there's a special kind of altar bread for people with celiac disease that has a very low amount of gluten." Father Mazi puts a hand on my shoulder. "Some religious sisters bake it in their convents. I can have Mrs. Gomez look into ordering some for our parish. It will be good to know we have an alternative available for people with the same condition or severe allergies. But it might take me a couple weeks to get the order in."

"Why can't they use rice?" I shrug the hand off. "I can't have any gluten. None at all. Zero percent."

He presses his lips together. "I hear you. But Church law says Communion has to contain at least point-zero-one percent of wheat," he says gently.

"Oh dear." Mrs. Gomez puts her hand on my shoulder. I shrug it off. "So what am I supposed to do?"

Father Mazi clasps his hands together. His calm voice says, "Well . . . if you don't want to try the sisters' altar bread, this will pose some logistical issues. You know at the eleven o'clock Mass I see you at, we only offer the Host; but at the nine-thirty, we have the option to offer both the Host and chalice. In fact, it's something I've wanted to do for our church for a while. We just need to train more extraordinary ministers. There it is! I will make sure we keep one chalice just for you to receive from, and I'll expect to see you bright and early on Sundays for now." He smiles as if this new idea solves everything.

Oh great. Another bonus point in the Latin Mass's favor was that I got to sleep in a little bit. Now that's going to change. Maybe I can ask Mom if we can go to the Saturday vigil. But then what if I ever manage to get another date?

I take a deep breath. "So that's what I'll do today? Take the chalice?"

Mrs. Gomez looks stricken. "We're celebrating the Novus Ordo today," she whispers, "but we were only going to offer the Host to the students. Maybe we can try to get another chalice and more wine. . . ."

Father Mazi looks at his watch. "No, we're already starting to run late. Gloria Jean, you just won't receive today."

Now, I, Gloria Jean Wisnewski, have *never* missed Communion. Because to miss Communion means either skipping church, which Mom would never let me get away with, even while on vacation, *or* it would mean I had sinned and hadn't gone to Confession. Just what would everyone think if I was the only one who didn't get Communion? What would Ian think?

"Gloria Jean?" Mrs. Gomez asks.

"Give me a minute, okay?" My brain feels like it's swirling down a drain.

"Alright, dear," Mrs. Gomez says. She puts on a mew face one more time before bustling back to the registration table.

Before Father Mazi can say something, I turn on my heel and walk past Connor, past the kids in my class, and out the back door. Want to know how I'm feeling now? My eyes are on fire, my brain has collapsed into this cesspool at the bottom of my throat, and I need to sit down before I gurgle it all back up.

Out in back of the building is a bench and a statue of Mary in a little garden. I sit there and start to yell in my head. If the sight or thought of Father Mazi didn't make me want to throw my shoe at him, I'd ask him if yelling in your head counts as prayer.

I'm trying to get this all straight. We're told God created people in his image. Okay, I don't quite get that, but for now, let's say I do. And celiac disease is something in my body. That God created. Now, about the rules. So God came down as Jesus to create the Church, which somehow started calling itself Catholic. And he made Peter "pope," even though they didn't call it that back then. And the Pope can make the rules because he's actually representing Jesus and speaking for God. Father Mazi should also know that I really think theology should come with a flow chart.

So, anyway, *why* would God have his Pope make a rule that says I can't receive Communion because of something about the way God made me? If Mrs. Fermacelli says we can understand God through our bodies, well how the heck can I do that if my body can't even *receive* Communion. Communion is God, right?

The back door opens, and Mrs. Gomez calls me in. I just can't go in there and accept and confirm my faith if I'm not sure I want to believe in something that makes me feel even worse than I already do. They're starting. I take one look at her and run for the garden gate.

VII

Thou shalt not
be Catholic,
or at the very least,
thou shalt be a very
bad one.

15

I don't stop running until I get to the drugstore five long blocks away from the hall. I hate how this town is so spread out and I can't get very far without a car. Inside, Olivia is trying on lip gloss.

"Hey," she says. She plumps her lip.

"Hi." I pick up a tube. *"Naughty Naranja."*

Olivia catches me in the mirror our faces try to share. She smirks. "That's for babies. Here, try this one."

I take the clear tube. *"Joie de Vivre."* More than I can afford.

"It tastes like champagne," Olivia says.

"What's in it?" The label is blank.

"Heck if I know. Whatever it is, it's irresistible to guys." After a pause, she snatches it from my hand.

I snatch it back. "Good. I think I might ask Kyle out."

Olivia glares at me. "You? Miss Innocent?"

This is not the Olivia from the locker room. "Jealous?"

She snorts a laugh. "Of *you*?" She shakes her head. "Good luck," she drawls. "Though that's a cute sweater. Got another hot date today?"

Self-consciously, I touch the camisole underneath my v-neck. Maybe I shouldn't have worn the little tank. But it seemed wrong somehow, going to a church thing without it. "Maybe. Actually, I just ditched out of Confirmation class. I'm tired of all the rules." I slowly roll *Joie de Vivre* up and down the palm of my hand. The churchy rules about Communion bread don't make sense, and are clearly not working for me. Maybe the churchy rules about relationships aren't for me, either. I consider peeling off the packaging on the tube, open it, and glide the gloss over my lips just to *watch* Olivia's face.

Olivia smacks her lips one more time. "Seriously? Didn't think you had anything like that in you."

The bell chimes and the sliding doors whoosh open. Of all people, it's Kyle. I also hate how this town is just small enough that we all have to run into each other.

I turn to Olivia. "Guess I do have good luck." I pretend to be super interested in the display of lip glosses, but straighten my back and do the flirty yoga pose. Now I really wish I hadn't worn the camisole.

"Guess you do," Her hair swishes away. But then she turns back and looks at me for a second, real serious, like with mom eyes. "Just don't let him show you the guest bathroom, okay?"

"Uh, okay." If *friends* don't even talk about the bathroom, why would a boyfriend? That is, if Kyle *wants* to be my boyfriend. I wouldn't mind. I think.

"Morning, Glory."

A weird tremble ripples across my back. If Kyle is to be my new non-churchy, soooo not a gentleman-gentleman boyfriend with *lots* of kissing,

1. He has to come up with a new nickname.

"Hey, Kyle. I was just about to try this gloss out. What do you think? I think it highlights the natural pink in my cheeks."

"Uh, you look hot."

2. He has a lot to learn about color.

"What I was going for." Oh, if Eden could see me now! Okay, she'd call me out for using a line from that movie, but still. "Let me get this and then maybe we can get lunch or hang out or something?"

He takes a hand out of his pockets and runs it through his hair. "Wow. What happened to you? Not playing shy anymore? " He looks to the left, then to the right, then takes the lip gloss and rolls it in his palm. After one final look over his shoulder, he slides his hand into his pocket. "I got this." And then he *takes my hand*.

Kyle Sneed is holding my hand. We are walking out of the drugstore. In his pocket, his left hand is holding stolen lip gloss, and in his right hand he is holding my hand. Kyle whistles as the bell chimes and the door whooshes.

We just stole. There is a commandment—number

seven, I think—"Thou shalt not steal." Kyle is breaking a commandment. I am helping him break the commandment. In addition to the now-familiar, hot, tingly feeling on my neck, my head is buzzing, and my stomach is queasy.

Kyle starts walking quickly, so I have to hurry, otherwise I feel like my arm is being tugged. Thank goodness he isn't looking at me, so I can take some deep breaths and try to calm down. Breaking this rule doesn't seem as exciting as breaking the others.

"We can get a panini at the café in the bookstore over there." He fumbles in his pocket. "Here. So you can touch up after." He winks. All of my skin tingles. I could get my first kiss today.

A panini sounds worldly. Connor probably could not spell or pronounce panini, I tell myself. I take the lip gloss and roll it around in my palm. Ian probably wouldn't steal lip gloss for me. I'm not sure if Connor would or not.

Thinking about Ian and Connor reminds me of the retreat. Mrs. Gomez must have called my parents by now. People are probably looking for me. But I am on a date with New Kid Kyle Sneed. Who seems to be the one who will give me my very first kiss. And who steals things. Even if I went back after lunch, even if I could have Communion, I wouldn't be able to take it. Because this whole thing is so very wrong.

Misty Parker said we make choices. And that they're only OH-KAY if we both agree we want to do them. But nothing about any choice I've made since leaving the rec hall feels OH-KAY. And my first kiss? It seems like it won't necessarily follow the four *f*'s. But why bother following that rule if the one about Communion doesn't seem to make any sense?

I smile at Kyle and quicken my pace through the shopping plaza. "What's good to try? I've never had one."

"Ham and cheese is good."

Ham and cheese is boring. Kyle is boring. When he's not trying to flirt, that is. Then he makes me all nervous, but in a sometimes good way, sometimes uncomfortable way. His lips aren't as full of Connor's, but he seems to be more clear about his intentions. And now I think I'm sure I want my first kiss to be with someone who definitely wants to kiss me.

The café is in the middle of a mega-sized bookstore. I want to roam around the art and fashion sections. Kyle likes listening to rap CDs in the music section. They only have one set of headphones at the listening station, so I'm stuck standing around while he bops his head.

The burnt-cheese smell of cooking paninis hovers over the café. I have lost my appetite. We take our sandwiches to a table in the corner and sit down.

Then I feel Kyle's foot traveling up my leg. I choke on the rubbery cheese and too-soft bread. I nearly gag.

Kyle draws his foot off my leg. "Right, not here." He winks.

I nod. Wait. Are we going somewhere else? Shouldn't we get to know each other better? I dab at my lips with a napkin. "Um, what's your favorite color?" I ask.

"Brown." Kyle's eyes wander around the café.

I take a long sip of water to mask my horror. That is my least favorite color. "Why?" I manage to say.

He shrugs.

I could tell him that my favorite is aquamarine because it's cool and happy and whenever I see it, I just want to dive in and float on my back. Ian's eyes are aquamarine.

I pinch myself. I am not supposed to be thinking of Ian. No more churchy guys, remember? I take a big bite of my panini. No more celiac disease either.

"My turn for a question," he says, leaning forward. "Want to get out of here? My sister gets off in ten minutes." He jerks his head back toward the girl running the espresso machine.

"Where would we go?" I hope he says the park. I see old couples there sometimes, holding hands and getting pecks on their cheeks. So sweet.

"My house. We've got the guest cabana." He wiggles his eyebrows and gives himself a Spanish accent. "And the hammock."

The hammock. The hammock Eden and Zack were sitting in. Kissing in. Below the table, my right leg starts jiggling.

"We could go swimming." He winks again.

"I . . . I don't have a bathing suit," I stutter. I press on my leg to stop it from bouncing.

Kyle leans forward. "You can borrow one of my sister's."

"Might be kind of big on me," I whisper. I tug on my necklace down to my camisole.

His eyes flick there. "The strings are adjustable. It'll be okay."

I swallow dry air. That would mean changing in a

bathroom. Bathroom. I kind of need one right now. And didn't Olivia say something about avoiding the bathroom?

"No. I don't know." Under the table, my hand clutches my stomach.

"Okay. No swimming. We've got the hammock and the cabana. And it's private. We could have a whole lotta fun with that lip gloss. It's not that sticky kind, either. Man, I hate that." He leans back in his chair all casual.

I sink further into my chair, increasing the distance between us. "I'm not sure . . ." My insides are cramping.

"No, I'm saying it's not. I've had it before." Wink.

Oh. *Oh*. He's kissed another girl who wears *Joie de Vivre*. Of course he has. He's kissed another girl period. Maybe even lots of girls. So this would only be special for me. Not for him.

"Ready, turd?" Kyle's sister stops by our table. "Who's this?"

"Gloria Jean. She's going to come over. We're gonna hang out."

"Does Mom know about this?"

"No, and don't tell her, okay?" Kyle has kind of a whisper and his voice cracks.

She laughs and rolls her eyes. "Right. Come on." She leads us to her car.

The cramps feel like a dozen writhing snakes. It's just like that time during the social studies test. Forget the cabana. And the hammock. I need to get out of here, quick.

"Gloria Jean! Are you okay?" It's Connor Riley jogging through the parking lot from the direction of the hall.

"What are you doing here?" It feels like the writhing

snakes are now biting me. I want to bolt from here, but I don't want him following me to the bathroom.

Connor's a little out of breath when he reaches the car. "We got a reflection period break. Mrs. Gomez and Father Mazi are going crazy trying to find you. I figured you wouldn't walk all the way home. And you're smart, so books. . . ."

Kyle's sister kicks her tire. "In or out?"

Connor is looking at me with nice eyes. Kyle has annoyed eyes. I bet he's picked up on the church stuff. I bet he sees right through my attempt to be in his league and sees me as just some silly girl who has no clue what she's doing. I bet he thinks Connor is a wimpy priest wannabe.

"Out."

They get in the car and drive away. I look at Connor. "I'll be right back. Stay here. Don't tell anyone, okay?"

I sprint to the bathroom, all the way at the back of the store. I'm not as long as I was at the movies. But still.

Connor is sitting on the sidewalk. "Are you sure you're okay? Like, that stuff about the hospital? Don't lie."

"Yes. I'm fine. I went to the hospital for a test. You really care that much?"

"I care." He shuffles his feet and looks down. "Itswhylaskedyouout."

"If you care so much, then why did you laugh at me?"

"When?"

"Kyle's pool party."

"I laughed?"

"Yeah."

"Wow, you have a good memory. Uhhh . . . oh! Because

Kyle was being a jerk. I don't think that's how you're supposed to ask a girl out."

"Oh, and how are you supposed to?"

Connor kicks at some gravel. "Seriously? You can remember the laugh but not a month before that? You said yes to the way I did it," he trails into a mumble.

My cheeks flush. Right. It was really cute. Last May when all the 7th graders went on a school science camping trip in the Everglades, the boys had pranked us pretty bad—they snuck into our tents and stole our underwear then hung them in the trees. So, led by yours truly, we girls took a bunch of fishing hooks and pinned the boys into their tents. Except Connor was coming back from the bathroom cabin. He pretended like he didn't see us. Then, after Eden had been talking a lot about her movie party at school, he finally came up to me one day after social studies, handed me a fishing hook and said "I kept this. From that time. Cuz I kinda had a crush on you. Still do. Want to go out with me?"

Now, in the parking lot of The Book Nook, I realize he's right, and I've been really, really stupid. Even though the date we went on didn't come with my first kiss. I nudge his shoe with mine. "Sorry," I whisper.

He stands, extends his hand and gently pulls me up. "We should get back to church," Connor says. But his fingers leave mine and go into his pockets.

I guess he's been reflecting all morning. But I've just started. On the five-block walk back, I consider the following:

1. Ian is nice. Ian is also Catholic.

2. Connor is nice, despite not kissing me. Maybe not kissing wasn't supposed to be mean. Connor is also Catholic, even if he doesn't go to church as often.

3. Kyle is not nice. Kyle is also not Catholic.

4. Maybe being Catholic, or having some set of rules or a code, really, makes Ian and Connor think about their choices and what makes them OH-KAY or not.

5. Maybe I need to give this whole faith thing another try. Because I am not nice. I have stolen lip gloss. I judged everyone in my Confirmation class. I judged Connor. And here he is finding me after I ran away, and being the ultimate gentleman.

We approach the building from the garden. Connor holds the door open for me. "You coming?"

16

Step one is into the main ballroom. Softly, the door closes behind me. Now I am frozen in front of it. Two high-schoolers are sitting on the small stage, giving a talk. I hear words like "prayer" and "relationship."

"They're going to start small group discussions soon," Connor whispers. "We're being put into groups of five according to which church we're from."

I nod. Once the talk is over, I'll join whichever group from my class has four. Wait. That'd be both. Whichever group Ian is in. *Oh*. I wonder if they split themselves into boys and girls.

Suddenly everyone uncurls themselves off the floor and heads to the tables around the hall.

"Gloria Jean!" Ian waves at me. "We're over here!"

Julian, Mary Bridget, and Angela also sit at the table. Slowly I make my way over, glancing over my shoulder for Mrs. Gomez and Fr. Mazi. A couple of the other religious ed teachers and some parents are milling around the back, setting up cookies and juice. I don't recognize them, so they might not know I'm the runaway rebel girl.

Gingerly I sit down on a plastic chair next to Angela. Julian is right across from me. "Mrs. Gomez is furious with you," he says.

Ian rolls his eyes and leans back in his chair. "Actually, I'd say she's more concerned than anything."

Mary Bridget turns to me. "Gloria Jean, are you okay?" She has a voice like a chipmunk, but a sincere chipmunk, at least. What would be the worst that could happen if I tell them the truth? The worst has already happened with Eden. Maybe I've just been trusting the wrong people.

"Yeah, I'm okay. I just found out I have this," I stop short on the "dih" sound. I'd rather not call it a disease. "condition that means I can't have wheat or anything with gluten for the rest of my life, so I can't take the Host. I can't take Communion."

Ian sits up straight and leans forward. "Really? Aw, man. What are you going to do?"

I shrug. "I dunno. I brought in some rice wafers, but Father Mazi says I can't use them. Apparently, Communion has to have wheat. He said that there are some nuns who bake them with really low amounts. I mean that's kind of crazy, like mail order Jesus."

Ian stifles a laugh.

I smile back. "Other churches that aren't Catholic use lots of different stuff—matzo, pita. They'd probably have no problem with something else—like corn chips or rice cakes. I can have those." I slump into my chair. "I just don't get it."

Julian rolls his eyes. "Don't get it? It's the *bread* of life, not the rice cracker of life!"

Ian shoots him a dirty look. Then he relaxes his jaw and turns to Angela. "Hey, do you know anything about this?"

Angela reaches into her bag and pulls out her cell phone. Peering down into her lap, she scrolls for an app. I look over her shoulder. "The Fingertip Catechism." She does a search for "Eucharist" and reads. "So far, all I can see is CCC 1412: 'The essential signs of the Eucharistic sacrament are wheat bread and grape wine.'"

I slump further into my chair. "That doesn't really explain *why*."

"*Oooooo.*" Julian is smiling. "Somebody's in *truh*-bull."

I look over my shoulder. Father Mazi has spotted me. All he does is crook his index finger back and forth.

"Thanks for trying, Angela. Better get this over with."

Ian looks up. "Bye, Gloria. It was good to see you."

Mary Bridget waves. "Feel better!" she squeaks.

I follow Father Mazi into a little lounge room. Mrs. Gomez is pacing around. "Gloria Jean!" she half-shrieks. She starts forward, but then stops and clasps her hands to her chest. I think maybe she wanted to give me a hug. Instead she half-sits on the arm of a chair. "Your parents are waiting in the parking lot." I nod. Father Mazi sits on a plush chair. I just stand and pick something to look at to avoid his face. I choose a little basket of tissues and whatnot. This must be the room brides use to get ready for weddings.

"Gloria Jean, what you did today is very serious," Father Mazi says. His voice is smooth, but solemn. "Not only were we very concerned, but this day retreat is an important—and required—part of your Confirmation program. You have already missed half of it. Your absence and return are also a source of distraction to all the other candidates who are making the retreat. I don't think it would be appropriate for you to stay for the rest of the day."

I can't look at him; I'm so embarrassed. Instead, I focus on his hands clasped together. "I'm sorry," I whisper.

Mrs. Gomez stands still with her hands folded. "Why did you leave, Gloria Jean? It's not like you to do something like that."

I shift my weight from leg to leg and look up at the ceiling. "I . . . I didn't," my hands start moving around in the air, as if I could catch the right words to use. "I was mad about the Communion thing. I didn't want to be the only one not in line." My voice peters out to a whisper. I look at the floor. Now I really will be out of the line.

"Okay," Father Mazi says quietly. "But what about running away was going to fix that?

My insides feel like jello. "I don't know," I blubber. "Nothing. It was stupid. Can I please go? You said my parents are waiting."

Father Mazi shakes his head. "Not quite yet. We still have to discuss how you're going to make up this retreat."

I almost fall to the floor. Missing the retreat, along with a few classes, was the reason I had to be "held back" from Confirmation last year. I really don't want to wait another year. "I can make it up? When is the next one?"

"There isn't another retreat, Gloria Jean. But, as you may know, Saint Josemaria Escriva now offers daily Eucharistic adoration."

Did I know this? I'm trying to remember. "At the moment, we don't have anyone covering the 4–5 p.m. slot on Thursdays." He presses his fingertips together. "The retreat is eight hours long, so how about for the next eight weeks, starting after Thanksgiving, you come spend some time with the Lord on Thursdays. Mrs. Gomez will be in the parish office. You'll have to check in with her when you come in, and stop by on your way out. She'll record your hours in a spreadsheet. Once I see you've done all eight hours, we'll talk about your experience. How does that sound?"

I exhale and let my shoulders sag. *Eight hours*? I don't have a choice. "Okay."

His lips break open into a broad smile. "I think you'll get a lot out of adoration, Gloria Jean. It might help you think through your emotions and process all the changes you're experiencing, and the adjustments you need to make." I'm not sure how anyone can 'get a lot out of' just sitting there for *eight hours*. I don't say anything.

Father Mazi clears his throat. "Maybe you remember the Gospel reading we get every year in the Easter season. The one about the two disciples traveling along the road after the crucifixion? They meet a man?"

Oh good. A homily. I shrug. Father Mazi doesn't seem bothered that I don't know.

"Well, along the way they talk about how Jesus, a great teacher who worked many miracles, had been crucified. It starts getting late, and they invite the man to share dinner with them. When they are ready to eat, the man breaks a loaf of bread, and it is then that the two travelers see that the man is actually Jesus—that Jesus is risen from the dead. I think the verse is 'and he was made known to them in the breaking of the bread.'"

I pick at a loose thread on the bottom of my dress. Where is he going with this?

"Try meditating on that when you arrive for adoration. I think it will be a good, quiet retreat for you, Gloria Jean, just sitting with the Body of Christ. I know it's always been time well spent for me." He nods encouragingly. "Anything else you'd like to discuss with me this afternoon?"

I shake my head.

"All right. You may go to your parents now."

I pick up my backpack and rise out of the chair.

Father Mazi stands, too. "But I hope to see you very soon."

I trudge out of the little room and to the parking lot where Mom and Dad are waiting in the car. Instead of listening to their lecturing, my brain zeros in on some of Father Mazi's last words. Sitting with the body. It reminds me a little of when Eden's grandpa died. She couldn't come over because her grandma and mom were making her and Sarai sit *shivah*, which she said was like the wake the night before Gigi's funeral. Sitting in the physical presence of a body that couldn't hear you, couldn't see you, and couldn't talk back to you. Adoration seems like the same thing. What's the point?

VIII

Thou shalt
close your eyes.
Better that you have
no idea that I have no
idea what I'm doing.

17

The scene at home is epic. Thundery clouds blow in at the back window, making everything even gloomier. Mom and Dad are standing, yelling, waving hands. I sit at the dinner table, focusing on the blustery afternoon beyond their faces.

Mom rests a hip on the barstool chair near the kitchen ledge. "Now, Gloria Jean. You're not going to get away without talking about this. Just what is going on with you?"

"Mrs. Gomez told you what happened." I don't look at her.

She swivels my chair with her foot so I have to face her. "I want to hear it from you."

I let my top half collapse onto the kitchen table. I let my stringy hair fall around my face. Maybe Mom will calm down and stroke it. I mumble into my elbow. "I walked to that little shopping plaza on Pelton, went to the drugstore to buy some new lip gloss, and then got a panini at The Book Nook. I just wanted some space." Without looking up, I fish around in my pocket for the *Joie de Vive* and set it on the table. It kinda doesn't make sense for me to have it now.

Mom doesn't come over. Instead, she lets out a long, low breath. "Well then. You got your space. You are grounded until Christmas."

My head snaps up. Seriously? I don't want her to think this upsets me as much as it does. "Fine. Not like Eden's calling or anyone's going to ask me to the winter dance." I kick a chair, and it slides toward the wall.

"Just as well," Dad says. He folds his arms.

Mom nods emphatically. Then, ever so slightly, her cheeks fall. "What do you mean, 'Eden's not calling?' Did something happen?"

I cross my arms tighter and look at the ceiling.

"Fine. Don't tell us." Dad says. "But whatever it is with Eden, you'll have to fix it at school. No phone. No Internet. No movies, no parties, no brunches till Christmas."

Mom starts to say something, but her face has fallen a little, like she might be just as sad about my breakup with Eden. She picks up my chin and holds it in her hand. Her voice is gentle, but firm. "I know it might seem harsh. But you were supposed to be at the retreat, and you left without anyone's permission. That's a serious thing. It's unsafe. I get that you were upset about the Communion thing. But storming off wasn't the way to deal with it. You need to talk stuff like this out with us. That's why we'll keep up the dessert chats after your Confirmation classes."

I jerk back from her. "What's there to say? It's an unfair rule that they won't change! No one can explain it to me!"

Mom sinks to the barstool. "A lot of things in life aren't fair. Besides, you can still have Communion! We'll just go to the nine-thirty Mass so you can receive from the chalice. We will check with the doctor, and then maybe when the right kind of hosts come in, we can see how much those affect you. It's not that a big deal."

"Yes it is!" My voice is like the thunder outside.

Dad sighs deep and long. He rubs his temples. "Look, we are trying to do everything we can to make this easier on you," he says tightly. "But what you did today makes it harder on us."

"Gloria Jean, do you realize how dangerous that was? Leaving the retreat and then eating that food? You could make yourself sick," Mom says sadly.

"I know! I went to the bathroom after. I'm fine now. What's one panini?" I cross my arms again.

"Cancer," Dad practically spits.

"What?" My arms fall to my lap. Could everything we were so scared of last year actually come true now?

"You heard Dr. Schmidt," Mom says, a hitch in her throat. "If you keep damaging your intestines, it can lead to digestive cancers, among other things. Celiac disease runs in families, and based on his history, the doctor thinks Poppa has it."

"So . . . so all those years of Gigi's bread and his . . . his Troubles. . . ." The sky is a gray blue that looks like nothingness.

"Yes." Mom's face isn't red anymore. She sits in a chair and leans forward. "I can appreciate how difficult it is for you to think now about forty or fifty years down the road. You're so lucky we caught this in time to stop anything worse from happening other than some extra trips to the bathroom. But if it helps you to stick to your diet, think of those effects before you have a panini." Mom comes over to me. She picks up the tube. "Or use trashy lip gloss." She slightly smiles at the last bit and sets it back down.

I swallow back a lump of tears. She and Dad don't even know about my run-in with Kyle. They believe I went by myself. "I'm really, really sorry." I hand her the gloss. "I don't want it anymore."

Heading into my room, I realize I don't want any of it anymore. The boys. The fights with Eden. Being a supergood Catholic. Being a super-bad Catholic. But I am suspended in a blue fog, trapped. I collapse onto my bed and sob, sob so hard the tears cover the pillowcase.

The next morning, Mom and Dad make us go to church super early. They take a pew near the back, which I don't get, because to be the first to get the chalice before everyone else and their glutenized lips, I have to sit up front. I start to kneel, but Dad clears his throat rather loudly. I furrow my brow at him. He jerks his head toward the back left, then goes back to his prayer. *Oh.*

Confession.

Oh. That's why Fr. Mazi asked if there was anything else I had to discuss. I do feel bad. And I don't want to not be in the Communion line *again*. I put my kneeler back up and walk over to the little room.

If Fr. Mazi recognizes my voice, he doesn't say anything. When I'm done, I find Mom and Dad in the front pew. I say my prayers. Mrs. Gomez comes over and whispers how this will all work today. Fr. Mazi will have an extra chalice on the altar for me—next week they'll be more prepared and have enough Eucharistic ministers to offer it on all the lines. Then she'll be over by the ambo, which is like a podium, and I go to her first. And we can do this every Sunday as long as I need. She explains it like it's so easy.

"Okay," I whisper. But it's really not. I think it will feel really hard.

18

When we get home, I go straight to my room. Even though I didn't manage breakfast before we left for Mass, I don't feel like eating lunch. I can still taste my sip from the chalice on my lips and still feel like the eyes of everyone at church are on my back. I throw off my red cardigan. What was I thinking wearing that color? Apparently I'd already drawn enough attention to myself with the chalice being offered. After I'd gone and went back to the pew, I couldn't help but look at everyone else in line, startled by Mrs. Gomez and the chalice. Like they were confused about what to do. Then, at the donut table, someone asked Mrs.

Gomez why, and she nodded in my direction and started to whisper to them.

I flop onto bed and lie there for a while.

"Gloria Jean, you have a visitor." Mom calls from outside my door. " Only five minutes. She's grounded," I hear her stage whisper.

"No problem, Mrs. Wisnewski. I'll be quick."

Great. It's Olivia.

"What?" I say when she gently opens and closes my bedroom door.

"Kyle wants his lip gloss back."

I fold my arms across my chest. "*His* lip gloss?"

"Yeah. He said yesterday he got you some lip gloss but then you totally blew him off for Connor."

"'Got' me lip gloss. Heh. He stole it."

Olivia rolls her eyes. "I figured. I came to get it back. I'll take it back to the store."

I relax my arms and sit on my bed. "Seriously?"

"I didn't want it eating away at your conscience or whatever."

Sighing, I say, "I already told my mom about it. We're taking care of it." Part of the penance Fr. Mazi gave me at confession is to either bring the gloss back to the store or pay for it. Mom is taking me there tomorrow.

Olivia nods. She looks away.

I go to open the door, but stop for a second. "When did Kyle tell you about the gloss? How does something like that even come up?"

Olivia sits in my desk chair and a leg bounces up and down. "Today . . . he didn't like mine . . . he liked the one he snagged for you. But you . . ." She shakes her head. She sounds like she's going to cry.

"Okay, just *what is* your problem?"

"Why are you asking so many questions? I'm the one who was going to do you a favor. Gawd." She swivels up and out of the chair. She swings open the door.

I slam it shut again and block it with my string-bean arms. "I think I've done more than enough for you. Not telling everyone how weird you are—mean in class, then crying alone. Talking about the bathroom. And, *and* you got Kyle. Isn't that what you wanted?"

Olivia's eyes look hard. She can't look at me. "You. Don't. Get It. With this stuff, you are so stupid. But actually, that is what makes you so smart."

My hand falls off the doorknob. I step aside a little, and Olivia tears down the stairs.

After she leaves, I sit at my desk for a while. I think about what we heard at Mass this morning. "Man cannot live on bread alone." Alone. That's how I've been feeling since finding out I have celiac. Some of it is not my fault. I didn't ask to inherit this disease or be the only one with a special dietary plan at the cafeteria or the one to cause new rules for the birthday bake binge. If our school has a kid with a peanut allergy or something, then maybe someone could relate. But I've never heard about one or met one. It's just me.

I go over to my dresser and face the mirror. It seems really empty without Eden filling the frame. My body and face haven't changed too much, except maybe I have less acne. What am I really unhappy about? Is it the rule about Communion? Or my body?

I think about the last Confirmation class. "Our bodies and souls are gifts from God, and chastity helps protect them," Mrs. Fermacelli had said. "Communion is like food for our souls," Miss Tompkins had said. Then shouldn't that mean it's all supposed to work together? But I'm different. To protect *my* actual body, I can't eat the "food for my soul." Okay, I do have the wine option. But I still want to know why wheat is so important. Why rice or corn chips or anything that works for me isn't good enough.

As I shuffle back to the desk, my hand knocks off one of my tubes of lip balm. I reach down to pick it up. I really hate this carpet. When J.P. went off to college, Mom decided I could re-do my room. Instead of keeping the light-gray Berber that came with the house, I could pick out my new carpet. I already had the bedspread picked out, which complemented the paint—and that took three weeks to pick out just the right shade of pale green. I had wanted aquamarine, so I could feel like I was sleeping in the ocean, but Mom said no. Blue would be too hard to paint over. Finally, finally, we had it all ready, but no carpet. Every sample clashed. Then, one night when I came home with Eden in tow for a sleepover, Dad had bought the solution. We needed a neutral color, but not white, because I couldn't keep it clean. He said the guy called it "cracked wheat." *Wheat.* It wasn't quite beige, and there were some flecks of brown. Eden said it looked like one big piece of matzo.

I can't keep thinking of Eden. Or things I can't have. Dropping the lip gloss, I instead reach for my back pack and pull out my sketches. This contest, *this* I could have.

The bright colors pop against the bland carpet. I grab an eraser and erase the faint line I'd sketched for a camisole on one of the dresses. Then I shade it again. There have to be better ways to stand out or get attention. It doesn't seem like Olivia's feeling too good about her way. And neither am I. I'm not sure what to make of all this right now. Whatever it is, I can figure it out later. I've got a contest to win.

The following week at school, I don't try talking to Eden, and she doesn't try talking to me. We only have three days this week, so it won't be awkward for too long. On Monday, in Social Studies, Mr. Gio reminds us about our term projects. No, I have no idea what topic I'm doing now. Alone. But I'll figure something out.

On Tuesday, in gym, we're doing basketball drills in pairs of two. I'm partnered with Olivia. We don't say anything, but the only thing bouncing are the balls. And her shorts seem longer.

Then, on Wednesday, a bunch of girls are crowding the office to hand in their design portfolios, to the secretary, who will submit them. Most are showing off their favorites, lots of cooing and oohing. From what I can tell, there's a lot of beach inspiration and stuff you can find in the juniors section in the mall already. I keep mine closed and simply drop it off at the desk. Olivia hangs back in the corner, clutching hers to her chest. She gives me a little smile. I don't know what this means, but I smile a little, too.

But then that brings us to Thursday. Turkey Day used to be my favorite holiday.

Cornbread stuffing drizzled with maple syrup. Homemade nutmeg crust for the pumpkin pie. Fried onions on top of the green bean casserole. J.P. and Dad and Poppa tossing the football to me on the empty street in front of our house. None of that now. J.P. stayed up at school so he could go to a big football game this coming Saturday. Poppa's at the nursing home. His cancer's back.

I still get my buttery mashed potatoes. We visit Poppa and try out a new gluten-free recipe to fake Gigi's bread. Mrs. Fermacelli, who is volunteering there, suggests asking Father Mazi to offer a Mass for him.

I had felt so happy for many years. Now, in the space of a few days, I just feel empty.

19

Monday brings a new month, which means more sex ed. Terrific. Even though we don't have to dress out today, Eden is in yoga pants. The really cute, cozy, eggplant-colored yoga pants I got her for her birthday and an oversized tunic sweater. Her chin is in her hands and her elbows are on her knees. I sit three rows up and four seats over.

"Bad weekend?" Melissa asks.

"Hmm?" I can't believe she's sitting next to me.

Melissa rifles through her bag. "You look all sad."

This is new. Is she actually concerned? I pick my head up from my hands and stretch out my legs.

"It was okay."

"Well, mine was awful. Eric didn't text me."

"Was he supposed to?"

"Uh, yeah. I thought he would have."

"Well, did he know that?"

"Yeah. I mean, shouldn't he? Geez, whose side are you on?"

I shake my head and sigh. This sounds more like normal. But it's not the normal I want. I finally look at her. "I didn't mean for that to be mean. Your time with Eric at the movies didn't go well, right? And I thought since Halloween you wanted to go out with Kyle."

Melissa nods.

"Maybe Eric didn't know you wanted him to still text you. Did you try texting him?"

Melissa shakes her head. "No. I didn't know I could."

"Eyes forward, eighth grade." Coach Nuñez and Coach Michaels are on the basketball court. The woman from before isn't there. Neither is the pizza box.

"Today you are getting into groups and learning about risk assessment. Sexual activity can have consequences, and those may differ. Each group will receive a set of flash cards." Coach Michaels holds up a deck of what looks like thick, over-sized index cards. "At the top of each card is the name of an act and consequences associated with that act. As a group, you will place the cards in order of lowest risk to highest risk. After twenty minutes, we will lead the discussion about the activity."

Several boys snicker. Eric and Kyle are nudging elbows and raising eyebrows at us girls.

Coach Nuñez puts her arm out in front of Kyle. "I will assign the groups for the girls, and Coach Michaels for the boys."

There are six cards. Each has an activity on it. Apparently "none of the above" is not an option. The tamest thing seems to be making out, but they don't call it that. There are more scientific words on the other cards. I can't believe they think we'd actually do some of this stuff. With ·its long list of consequences, I guess we're supposed to put the card that represents going all the way as the riskiest option.

Melissa sighs audibly and starts chewing her hair as she stares at the cards.

"Hi." Eden gingerly climbs up the steps.

"Hi, Eden."

"Coach put me in a group with you and Melissa. How are you?"

"Fine."

"How's all that stomach stuff?"

"Fine. I guess."

"So nothing's wrong?"

"Just my diet."

"What do you mean?"

"No gluten."

"Oh. Well, that's not too bad, is it?"

"Uh, well . . . it's in a lot of stuff, stuff you wouldn't even think of. Weird stuff, like envelope glue. And ham."

"Oh, well, I can't have ham, either! I get it. I mean, I have to keep kosher. Like, I would looooooove a cheeseburger. You could still have one. Just, you know, without the buns."

"It's different. You've *decided* to keep kosher. I am not medically allowed to eat it. Ever again. I can't have most types of cake. Practically no cookies. It's even in some brands of lip gloss."

"Oh my GAWD!"

"Oh! Don't get me started on that. I can't even have Communion at church the usual way."

"What? I mean, I don't know much about what Catholics do at church, but I know that's like a big deal, right?" Eden looks genuinely horrified.

"Like the biggest."

"Oh, Glorie Jeanie. What are you going to do?" Her voice is really small.

"I can have the wine," I say cheerily. Maybe if I tell myself I'm okay with this, I'll actually get to being okay with it.

Eden puts on the mischievous grin she wore every time she visited me when I was sick last year. "You should tell Olivia that. Might make her jealous."

I shake my head. Something about the way Olivia was acting tells me she wouldn't be impressed that I get a sip of watered down, bad-tasting wine once a week. And using something religious and medical to one-up her doesn't make me seem as smart as she thinks I am.

It feels a little weird to be actually caring what Olivia thinks of me. And even weirder that Eden doesn't seem to get it. Or has she never gotten it? I mean, that day in class when I ran to the locker room, who was there for me? Not Eden.

"It's actually really annoying. It makes me different."

"I'm different, too, you know." Eden's voice is light. It's obvious that she's trying to be reassuring. She lightly touches my arm. My muscles tense. On the one hand, I want us to be connected again. And I appreciate her rallying right now, even though it's kinda late. But something about this past month makes me think we won't be connected—at least in the same way—ever again. And it's not just about the diet.

"Yeah, well your religion says it's the law to *not* eat things. Mine says it's the law *to eat* the one thing that makes me sick. Sure, I have a different thing to take, but it's still different. I have to go up in front of the whole church first because I can't risk picking up gluten left by someone else's mouth. Everyone looks at me. Plus we have to go to Mass at a new time for a while, and the music is retro in a bad way at that Mass, and it's *so early*."

Eden's face crumples. "That is really bad. I'm sorry."

"Yeah. It stinks."

"No, Gloria. I am really, *really* sorry." Her voice is quiet and tender, like it was the time she came to Gigi's funeral and whispered in my ear that she would help me get through this. Evidence #4 we thought we were soul mates: both of us know what it's like to lose grandparents.

"Not just about this. For everything. I shouldn't have blown you off for Zack. I should've been there more for you. I should have called. But I just kept waiting for you to call me."

"And I was doing the same thing."

Melissa starts giggling uncontrollably.

"What?" Eden and I say at the same time.

"We're all so stupid. Like, unbelievably, ridiculously stupid," she says. She looks up. A pair of tall legs has joined our group. "What do *you* want?" she asks them.

The legs belong to Olivia. "Coach says I hafta be in your group. And after this activity, she's going to tell us about the presentations we have to do after break."

"Well, just so we're clear, this is our group." Eden motions her hand around our circle of three.

Olivia runs her tongue over her teeth and looks away. She picks up her bag and stomps off.

"What'd you do that for?" I ask.

Eden gives me a "what the heck" look. "She's a witch-with-a-b. I'd rather figure all this out with you two, even if she already has personal experience with this stuff."

"What's that supposed to mean?"

"Didn't you hear?" Melissa asks. "Last year, at some party, Olivia gave some boy exactly what he asked for."

"You mean . . ." Eden says, pointing to a card that I guess might belong somewhere in the middle of the stack.

Melissa nods and goes back to twirling her hair, like this isn't the biggest, saddest news of the period.

I look down at the pamphlet that came with the deck of cards. The last page lists FACT and FICTION. In bold font, one "FICTION" stands out: "Most teenagers have had sex or are telling the whole truth when they talk about their sexual experiences."

"How do you know?" Eden asks. "Do you know who the guy was?"

Melissa shrugs. "Dunno. Only heard it from my older sister, who told me she hoped I didn't become a slut like O."

I want to vomit, but this time, it's not because of something I ate. At the beginning of the semester, Coach Nuñez had a special Lady Boot Camp to start the health class part of gym. We learned about her rules. And then we came up with our own—the codes. We also learned her policy on cussing. Of course we couldn't say the usual words. But we also weren't supposed to call each other her own list of forbidden words. Melissa has just used the "s" word.

I don't think Olivia is a slut. I just think she puts on a front because that's all she knows.

Eden doesn't seem to think this is a big deal, either. "So how long do you want to give it before she goes after Kyle?"

I really don't like the direction this conversation is going. Maybe that's what Olivia's mysterious comments about bathrooms and her crying in the locker room were about. If she did something with Kyle that is on one of these cards, then Coach Nuñez said we shouldn't be broadcasting it. No, I definitely won't tell the girls this. While I don't get why Olivia's trusting me at all, I won't share her secrets behind her back. That's just a rule every girl should know. So I change the subject.

"Kyle and I went out."

Melissa spits out her hair. "*What*?"

"*What*?" Eden whisper shrieks. "You waited this long to tell me?"

It's been all of thirty minutes that we've been back together.

"I ran away from my Confirmation retreat. He

shoplifted lip gloss from the drugstore, took me to The Book Nook, and tried to get me to go home with him."

"So did you?" Melissa asks eagerly.

"NO! He's actually pretty skeevy. I don't like him. It's like all he wants is one thing."

Eden cocks her head. "Well, then he and Olivia are perfect for each other."

Melissa nods.

They're not. I think Olivia feels guilty and doesn't know what to do about it. Maybe that's why she talked to me. She thinks I know what to do. The problem is, I don't.

"What if it's all an act, and Kyle is just making it up? Maybe he thinks that's what's hot." All this talk about judging people we hardly know is making me uncomfortable. Maybe Kyle is feeling the same as Olivia. "I mean, has he actually gone out on a date with anyone?" A real date, I mentally add. Not shoplifting and not hiding in some cabana.

Melissa scratches at the pamphlet with her pen, the paper as frayed as her split ends. "Not that I've heard. But what does that matter? We've actually gone out with guys. Guys who seemed nice. And look where that got us. Nowhere. And probably never again. Even if it is an act, at least he knows what he's doing."

Eden puts her hand on Melissa's. "Aw. Don't worry. You'll get a real kiss soon."

Melissa shakes off Eden's hand and flicks at the bracelet Zack gave her. Eden frowns and turns away. Knowing how she feels, I put my hand on Melissa's. She lets it stay for the rest of the period. We copy each other's answers and fill up the worksheets, but we say nothing, because we're clueless.

For the rest of the week my day planner fills up with mental notes on lunches:

Tuesday: Gluten Free cupcakes—cheap-chocolate-tasting sludge that sticks in my mouth like peanut butter. Melissa and Eden still aren't speaking to each other.

Wednesday: Grapes for dessert. And the string cheese makes me sick. Eden holds my hair back while I hang over the toilet and she skips out on meeting Zack in the gym.

Thursday: "The expensive ham" ham roll-ups with corn tortilla chips and dipping salsa. Mom must have gotten up early to make the lunch. In a good enough mood to comfort Eden after her and Zack's very public argument in the main hall during class change.

After the final bell rings, I stay in the social studies classroom to use the computers and try to come up with a Gio project. Mom will pick me up here and drive me to do my adoration hour, which I'll do before Confirmation class. It's going to be a really long night.

I stumble across this one site called "Random Fact, Random Fiction." An article title about wine catches my eye. I start reading, and apparently, long ago, like Jesus's time long ago, in areas far from lakes, it was more common to drink wine than water. Hmmph. I try to find something about how they made bread back then. No luck.

When Mom comes to get me, we say nothing the

whole ride to the church. I still can't believe I have to do this. No one else does. I wonder if any of the kids in my class will say anything if they see me coming from the church to our room.

Inside, I pick a pew in the center. The kneeler comes slamming to a floor with a thud. The older woman sitting near the front turns and glares at me. Great.

I close my eyes and run through all the prayers I know. When I open them again, the woman is gone. I sit back and tap my feet against the kneeler. I look at my cell phone. A grand total of 7 minutes have passed. Now what?

There was that Gospel story Fr. Mazi was telling me. "Made known to them in the breaking of the bread." Well, that's just perfect. There was no "made known to them in the pouring of the wine," now was there? I mean, the Host is so familiar. I'm not sure anything else will ever seem like Communion to me. The bright red hymnal catches my eye. Don't most of the Communion songs refer to "wheat" and the "Bread of Life"? Yup. Not a whole lot about the "wine of life." I shut the book with force and drop it to the pew.

Sighing, I face the altar. Even adoration is focused on the bread. No one sits and adores a clear chalice, now do they?

WHY? I scream in my head. *Why*? The pressure in the back of my head builds and I feel hot all over. I ball my fists. . . . Why?

Breathing deeply, I remind myself that I have class after this, and can't be all blotchy. I bow my head down and focus on the bench of the pew until the feeling passes. Mom never likes it when I whine. I can't imagine God does, either.

Whine.

Wine. Then, out of nowhere, I somehow remember that Gospel story of the wedding, when Jesus turned the water into wine. We're supposed to focus on the fact that it's his first miracle. What if that event gives the wine more meaning? Like the article said, water could be so scarce in some areas. And then if this important family didn't have any wine for their guests, they'd be really embarrassed. Probably as embarrassed as someone who has to go first in Communion line. So Jesus took the plain water and changed it, made it something new.

Maybe that's what needs to happen for me, too. Be changed. Be made new. But how?

I try to think about that the rest of the time. Later, when everyone starts coming into the classroom, Hallie and Hanna come up to me.

"Hey, Gloria, Jean!" Hanna says. "Hi!" Hallie chirps.

"Hey." I shrug.

Hallie leans close over my desk. "Okay, so don't get mad, but we heard about your . . .

" . . . what's going on with you," Hanna finishes. "And we wanted to let you know you're not alone."

Hallie smiles. "Yeah, there's a girl at our school who has it."

I lean closer. "Really?"

Hanna nods eagerly. "Uh-huh. So, don't get mad, but we were thinking of you and asked her how she deals with it all."

"Oh yeah?" I say all casual. I don't want them knowing how much this interests me.

"Yeah!" Hallie says. "She was diagnosed when she was a little kid and even got teased a lot."

"Yeah," Hanna breathes. "This one time a little girl freaked out when she wanted to take a cookie she was offering to everyone else and told her she was gross because she had a disease."

How awful. "What'd she do?"

"Well," Hallie says. "She told her mom, and her mom said it was okay if she was unhappy, but if she let others know that she thought it was a bad thing, they'd act like it was a bad thing."

"So she just had to pretend she was happy around everyone?"

Hanna and Hallie nod encouragingly. "Yup. She says her mom was right. The more she acted like she was okay with everything, the easier it got to feel that it really was okay."

A smile starts to form on my lips. "Fake it till I make it? Okay. What'd she do about church?"

"Oh, I don't think she goes," Hallie says.

I shrink back into my seat. Miss Tompkins calls us to attention. My mind starts to wander, and I let it. You can't fake faith, can you?

IX

But thou shalt
look into my eyes
right before. That way
I know you're seeing
the whole me—
faults and all—and
still think I'm okay.

20

After Confirmation class, Mom takes me to the dessert place. I'm all set to read the menu when Mom swats it down. Smiling, she motions for a waiter to come over and then whispers into his ear. Five minutes later, he sets a plate down in front of me.

Mom nods encouragingly.

Haltingly, I take a couple of bites. Immediately I spit them into my napkin. "Blech! What is this? It's awful! Let me get something else."

"But Gloria Jean, I called the chef and told him and he made this special. . . ." Mom's voice is kind of whiny.

I don't care. I slide my chair back, stand up, throw the linen napkin on the table, and stomp off.

"Gloria Jean!"

I go outside and stand by the car. How dare she! How dare she *call* up the chef, some guy I don't even know, and tell him all about my digestive issues so I can have a gross-tasting cake!

Mom storms over to the car, her oversize purse swinging wildly. She unlocks the door. I climb in and start to kick off my shoes.

"Feet down, Gloria Jean." Her voice means business.

"Fake it 'til I make it," I whisper.

"What?" She refuses to start the car.

"I'm sorry," I say quietly.

She sighs. "Me too." She turns the key in the ignition.

On the way home, we don't say a word. I want some control over this situation, over all situations. The irony (another vocab word) is that I've gone *waaay* out of control. Maybe I should come up with rules for Mom and Dad.

I lie on the matzo carpet to do my homework. The social studies project rubric glares at me from my binder. Matzo is the special bread Eden and her family eats at Passover. So another religion has a focus on food. Something in my head clicks. The Eucharist is Jesus's body given up for all of us, right? And we're supposed to be thankful that he's made this sacrifice. Miss Tompkins said we're meant to sacrifice too. Maybe this disease is like a built-in system for sacrifice, and it's up to me to figure out how to make it worthwhile. Maybe knowing more about what I'm giving up will help.

I head downstairs to ask permission to use the computer. I finally have a social studies project topic: the cultural history of bread. Dad nods encouragingly.

* * *

The next afternoon, the principal, Mr. Tourley comes on the PA and crackles that I should report to his office. Eden whips her head around to look at me. Her eyebrows ask, "What's going on?" I shrug. Everyone goes "*Oooooo.*" Now I, Gloria Jean Wisnewski, have *never* been called to the principal's office, so I'm not even exactly sure what to do.

I slowly get up from my desk, and once I'm out of the classroom, I hightail it down the hall. What could he want with me? When I get into the office, I nearly fly into Nurse Robben.

"Well, this is a surprise! Gloria Jean, how are you?" Nurse Robben beams. "I haven't seen you in so long!"

I shuffle from one foot to the other and peer around her shoulder to the principal's door. "Oh, I'm a lot better now." I beam back at her. "Thanks."

Nurse Robben's shoulders roll down into a satisfied sigh. "Good. I have to say that as much as it was a pleasure helping you, I'm so glad you don't need it anymore."

I shrug into myself, like I'm receiving an invisible hug. "Me too." I point to the door. "I gotta go in."

"Okay, I won't hold you." She passes to my left. "*Ooooooo,*" she says real low with a wink.

When I open the office door, I see Olivia already sitting down. Mr. Tourley motions for me to do the same.

"Well, ladies, I am just so pleased to give you this

news. You two have placed in the Young Designers competition. Ms. Wisnewski, you have placed third in the county."

Third!

"And Ms. Calamatto, you have won!"

Won!

Olivia grins sheepishly. I swear she looks like a five-year-old who's been told she's getting a pony. "I did it? I won?"

Mr. Tourley nods. "As regional winner, your designs will be featured at the Sable Palms SoFash store. Not only will you get a $100 gift certificate to the store, but you're also in the running for the statewide competition. And that lucky young lady gets a prize of six weeks at a fashion design summer camp. They will announce that winner after the holidays. Congratulations!"

Olivia sinks to a chair and hugs herself a little. I put a hand on her shoulder.

"Ms. Wisnewski?" Mr. Tourley beams at me. "For coming in third, you will receive a $50 gift certificate to SoFash." He hands me a manila envelope. "In just a few minutes, I'll show your designs as part of the closing announcements broadcast. You ladies may return to class now."

Olivia bounces up, her eyes as shiny as her hair. For once I don't judge her. This time, her experience will open new doors—better ones.

I'm okay with not winning it all. With everything going on, if I made it all the way and won the state contest, I don't know if heading off to a camp would be a good thing.

I would need to have special meals. And what would girls in Florida do with a coat with ruffles? But still. Clothes and color will always be a part of who I am, something that makes me special—kiss or no kiss.

When I get back to Gio's class, I flash Eden a thumbs up.

Five minutes before the bell rings, Mr. Tourley crackles on the PA, this time to the whole school, and directs us to turn on channel one. A cheesily designed slide announces my name and my placement. Then they show my designs. Eden turns around, tears pooling in her eyes. "Glorie Jeanie," she mouths. "Keep watching," I whisper. And smile.

Everyone gasps when they see the slide proclaiming Olivia's name next to the word "Winner!" And then I gasp loudest of all when I see her outfits. She's designed pretty, modest dresses. Like, seriously sweet with soft colors, hems that go to the knees, and necklines that don't show anything.

"I could actually wear that to church," I say out loud.

"Wow," Eden says. "Sorry you didn't win it all."

I shrug. "It's still pretty awesome!"

I wrap my arms around her from behind.

She leans her head back to look at me. "But it still would've been cool to get one of your looks made and put on display."

I shrug again.

"Now Olivia's going to be in the limelight. Again."

I look down at her, my voice light. "But at least this time it will be for something other than boys."

The intercom buzzes again. "And don't forget—we still have tickets on sale for the winter dance."

The bell rings three times. Eden and I are giggling as we pick up our books. Connor stops by.

"Yes?" Eden trills.

He looks at his brown boat shoes. "Uh, nothing." He looks back up at me. He smiles. "Have a good weekend. And congrats again."

I smile back. "Thanks!"

✳ ✳ ✳

"Bethlehem means 'house of bread.'" This little line from Fr. Mazi's homily at Sunday Mass won't leave me. Mary and Joseph were going to the town called the house of bread. It was always meant to be Jesus's hometown. Jesus is the "bread." So I get why the Host is supposed to be bread. But bread can be made of barley or potato or corn, so the bigger question remains—why *wheat* bread?

After Mass, I run into Ian at the coffee and donut table where I'm getting some tea. "Ian! What are you doing here? I thought you usually went to the Latin. . . ." *Oops*! Is it stalkerish of me that I know that? And said it aloud?

His head shrinks into his shoulders like the most adorable turtle. "I wanted to see y—see what it was like."

The warm tingles are back, but this time they're in my stomach. I think he was about to say that he wanted to see me! "And?"

He shrugs. "It was okay. The music wasn't the same. But the lyrics aren't bad." His long, tan fingers stroke his chin. "And I miss the Gloria." His smile is full, but not open, and forms these small, perfectly round, lightly pink cheeks.

The tingles are everywhere. Speak, Gloria Jean! But it's hard to make my lips move. My brain is full of bubbles. "Me too."

Stupid, stupid, stupid.

He grins and his eyes crinkle. "Well, maybe we should plan to go to Midnight Mass on Christmas Eve. It'll be worth the wait."

I cannot breathe. Air has stopped coming in and out of my lips. Yes it will, yes it will, yes it will.

"Gloria Jean!" Mom has left the grown-up half of the donut table.

"See you around, Gloria," he says. He turns to go, but then he looks over his shoulder. Is he going to wink? No! his beautiful blue eyes lock onto mine and hold their gaze. He blinks with long lashes and a small smile rises with his eyelids. Then he turns on a heel in a little spin and joins his parents and brothers and sisters near the door.

I practically faint into a startled Mom. "We have to go to Midnight Mass this year," I sigh dreamily.

All the way home I think about how maybe, just maybe, if we sit together at Midnight Mass, he might try to hold my hand during the Our Father.

21

For the whole week, I am deep into research mode. On Wednesday, Eden and Melissa come over and teach me how to make matzo and tortillas, and together we figure out how to prepare naan, this recipe from Mr. Dipthi, the science teacher. When I have to work with the batter, I wear these special gloves Dad bought me. We record making the recipes on my phone, so I can have cooking videos for my project.

Melissa heads home as soon as the dishes are done. Eden and I go up to my room. She stretches like a cat on my carpet. She picks a loose thread and studies it. "It's kind of funny, you know? Last summer I was calling this the matzo carpet, and today we made matzo."

I lie on the floor so I face her. "It's not funny. It's actually pretty cool. It's like even more evidence we were meant to be best friends." Evidence #5 to be exact.

"How so?"

"Well, both of our faiths have rules about what we should eat. And both of us have to eat unleavened bread." I pull at the loose thread. "I'm sorry if I made you think the choice to keep kosher wasn't that serious. This project has me thinking about food a lot."

Eden scrambles to her knees. "Ohmygosh, GJ, don't apologize. I'm sorry." Her voice has a hitch in it. "Helping you with this project has *me* thinking a lot. It must be really hard not to have a choice at all."

I sit up. I open my arms. "But I do. I can either accept the rules I need to live by to stay healthy or just keep being mad. And I don't want to be mad anymore."

"Now that is an OH-KAY choice." She falls into my arms and we share a great big hug.

After she leaves, I scour the Internet for the answer to the big question—why wheat? One thing I know is that it's found almost everywhere and can grow easily. I guess it's pretty cool that God could provide for people, but it's still a little crazy that it just has to be something that more and more people are allergic to.

When Mom drops me off at the church the next night, I feel more prepared this time, because I have something to think about. At first, I was so panicky at the thought that I would never have Communion ever again. And then when I learned I could, I just got mad about the way I had to take it, because I wanted to focus on what was fair. But here is the Eucharist waiting for me. After thinking about bread all week and the way it feeds so many different cultures, I kind of understand why the Church sees it as important.

Looking at the Host on the altar, I realize this is way different than a *shivah* or a wake. Those things are for dead bodies. And my faith teaches that the Body of Christ is alive. I mean Jesus did die, but he rose again. "Fake it 'til I make it," I whisper. I look forward at the Eucharist.

"Why?" I whisper. "Why this rule?"

I mean, I know life is full of rules. And there's the commandments. They're never really any fun. But they're important. They help the world make sense. And they protect. If Olivia and those guys followed any kind of rules on love and responsibility, maybe things would be different.

When I go to fill out my hours sheet in the office, I run into Julian's mom, who's getting buying some candles from Mrs. Gomez for her wreath. Oh yeah. It's the season of Advent. That means the coming of Christ. Even though he was born more than two thousand years ago, we still are supposed to wait with joy for him to come into the world in new ways. I feel like my whole life's an advent. Waiting for my first kiss. Waiting to stop feeling younger than I actually am. Waiting to stop looking younger than I actually am. Advent lasts only four weeks. I think Christmas might not come to my lips for forty years.

Ian is the first one in the classroom. "Hi, Gloria," he says. His voice is smooth and thick, like honey.

"Hi." I choke back a gulp. Does he remember sort of asking me out to Midnight Mass?

"How'd that contest go?" And then it cracks.

"I—it—wait, what? You remembered that?" The volume of my voice has dialed down.

"Yeah." Ian looks down, but I can see the corners of his lips lifting up those perfect cheeks. His eyes look up to mine. He clears his throat.

I shiver a little bit and wrap my arms around my chest to make it seem like I am actually cold. "I came in third."

"Aw, I'm sorry. Thought you would've won it all." He removes his hands from his pockets and leans forward a little, but then balls them up and rocks back on his heels.

"It's okay. The right person got what she deserved." I grin warmly.

"Miss Tompkins says we're going to try doing our opening prayer Ignatian style."

I giggle. "Always something new in this class, isn't there?"

He nods. "There's a spot next to me. I mean, if you want." His head points the way.

I nod encouragingly.

Once everyone else arrives, Mrs. Fermacelli has us push back the desks and sit on the floor for the prayer. She starts the prayer by reading a Scripture passage from Isaiah. I close my eyes. I try picturing myself in the story, but all can think of is Ian next to me. His hand is right there. I scrunch my fingers in, then send them out over the tile. My pinky almost touches his pinky. Suddenly, his slow, even breaths are louder than Mrs. Fermacelli's voice.

Then for some reason I suddenly think of Connor. How he held on to that moment from camping last year. Ian and I have never been camping. Is it okay that we just have seen these tiny pieces of each other and I want want *want* Ian to be my boyfriend? Does he want me in that way, too? Was he really flirting, or just being a nice guy? Can I ask? Does he want to know me better?

"Now class." Mrs. Fermacelli nudges the sole of my shoe lightly. "We're going to list how we think the gifts of the Holy Spirit work in our day-to-day lives. After you've made your list, discuss with a partner."

My list:

Courage: Ask Ian out. Or maybe Connor.

Knowledge: Figure out what I'm supposed to do with my hands when kissing.

Wisdom: Know the difference between Ian and Connor.

Understanding: Understand how this gift is different from knowledge or wisdom.

Piety: Not think about Ian or Connor in Confirmation class.

Fear of the Lord: Oh. I think if you fear the Lord that implies that you've thought about the Lord. Haven't been doing too much of that in this exercise.

Right Judgment: Make the right choice. Oh. I think I get it. There are a lot of choices I can make, and a lot of them are OH-KAY. But they're *just* okay. Maybe I need to think more about finding the RIGHT choice. And for some of the decisions lately, it's clear there are only two: chastity or not; accepting how Jesus comes to me or not. But with the boys, whom do I pick? Does it have to be A or B? Or can I pick all of the above—at different times of course? Maybe the not just okay, but RIGHT choice is none of the above.

Hanna and Hallie scoot over toward me. "Want to be in a group?" they ask. I look up. A curl falls onto Ian's forehead. He's still scribbling a lot.

"Sure." Might as well start now. But I can't really share these answers. My shoulders droop. Most are about kissing or boys.

Hallie goes first. Then Hanna. They list normal things like doing better in school or how they might fix some friendships that have gotten icky. Then they also have some things that sound holy. Going to adoration more.

I say I want to do that, too. And it hits me again just how angry I've been about the whole Eucharist thing. Every Sunday Mrs. Gomez beckons me with her hand, like you'd motion for a puppy. I never need to put on blush before Mass anymore. The embarrassment colors my cheeks just fine. It also doesn't help that Fr. Mazi has told other people at church that I'm the reason St. Josemaria's now offers the chalice to everyone at all the English Masses. I get a lot of isn't-she-precious smiles, and the old guys clap my Dad on the back, saying he's got quite the girl.

But adoration. Right now, I have to do it. But it doesn't seem so bad. I actually like the quiet. My head feels clearer. And I feel calmer. And it doesn't seem so hard to think of answers to the questions I have. And I'm still getting the Eucharist, just in a different way. Maybe this works for the whole kissing thing, too. If I'm not so focused on what

I can't have, maybe when I relax, it'll come in a way I didn't see coming.

"Yeah, more adoration—the whole 'fear of the Lord' part, because like Mrs. Fermacelli said, it's not being scared, but in awe, and more trying to figure out what grace God wants to give me this new year," I say to the girls. So much for my obsession with lip gloss. I suddenly realize that I was so focused on preparing my lips that I didn't even know who I was preparing them for. I still don't.

By now Ian has moved across the room to partner with Julian, who I bet has listed reading the *Catechism of the Catholic Church*, which looks like a brick, over vacation as his resolution. I think about how I came up with my resolution all by myself, and it wasn't to impress a boy. It was to name something authentic (new entry for life's vocabulary homework) that I want for myself.

Thankfully Monday brings regular gym class. It's cold outside, and not enough of my classmates have long-sleeved shirts and pants to dress out in. So we do barefoot stretches in groups in the gym. Boys on one side. Girls on the other.

Olivia exhales and comes out of standing stretch pose. She picks up a soft wrap-style jacket.

I walk over to her and get into warrior pose. "Hi. Congratulations again on the design contest!"

Olivia smiles. "Thanks."

"You excited about maybe getting to go to that camp?"

She nods. "People from the fashion industry will be the mentors. They come in from New York City. The camp's in Connecticut."

I think of Eden's trips up north and Mark. I don't know what else to say to her, so I say, "I hear the guys up there are cute."

"There won't be any guys. Girls only." She only smiles a little bit, but the gold in her hazel eyes blazes like she's really happy. "I'm more excited that I might get to go out of state. Never been before."

"Cool. I really did like your designs. Honestly, they were kind of a surprise." I switch the legs I'm extending so I don't have to see her face.

"I just draw what I want. What I think looks good. Like what you wear."

"Oh! Well, thanks." I relax out of the pose and sit down. I think back to this summer. I once saw her at the movies with her sister. She wore really short shorts and a tube top. "You ever shop at Modelly? That's where I go."

She settles into a seated pose and holds her feet. "No. My sister says that it's for little girls. And she likes to help me shop for what she says boys will think looks good."

"Ah. Well. Maybe after the award ceremony at SoFash, we can head over there and look."

"Yeah. Maybe." Olivia lies down and stretches her arms out way over her head.

I start to head back toward my mat, but Olivia's small voice still dings in my head. I sit next to her head. "Hey."

"What?" Her eyes don't open. The small voice is gone. She's annoyed.

"We've got those gift certificates to SoFash. I think they sell some make up there. Maybe we can both get new lip gloss. You know, since we didn't get *Joie de Vivre*."

"I don't want it anymore." She opens her eyes. The small voice is back. "No matter what people say—and trust me, I know what you all say about me—I never really wanted it at all."

I stare straight ahead. We're not talking about lip gloss anymore. She means the boy at that party. And Gross Kid Kyle Sneed. I gently brush away the wisps of hair that have fallen over her forehead.

"Not doing those things again is a choice, too. And that is OH-KAY. Like the most OH-KAY choice."

Olivia starts giggling at my horrible Misty Parker impression. "Good."

I head back over to my mat. Eden and Melissa are stretching. "Everything cool, Gloria Jean?"

"Yup. I'm thinking we should put Olivia in our group for the sex ed presentation thing."

"Really?" Eden cocks her head.

I nod. "I think she acts the way boys and other people think she should. I think her designs show that she wants something different. But we haven't been giving her a chance."

Melissa bites her lip. "I have never seen her be nice to other girls. Only the guys." She chews on a lock of hair. "But we haven't exactly been nice to her."

Eden bounces up. "Let's start."

And with that, Olivia is in our group. And we know exactly what our topic is going to be: How to Protect Your Heart.

Later that afternoon, in social studies, Eric and Connor are doing their presentation. It's a podcast on the cultural history of the weird explanations of some of the wonders of the world. Did aliens build the pyramids; what happened to Atlantis; what's the deal with Stonehenge. That sort of thing. It's really neat. Connor speaks in a funny deep baritone voice throughout the whole thing.

When they're done, I clap really loudly. "That was really cool, even if it wasn't soccer," I whisper when he passes by my desk. He smiles at me and blushes. Yes, I remembered from the not-a-date-date.

"Yeah," he whispers back. He bends down like he's tying his shoe. "Eric really wanted to do this idea, and he likes to get his way."

Five seconds later, he flicks a note at me from his desk. "Want to go to the dance with me?"

Next presentation: fireworks.

X

Thou shalt
only do it if you
really mean it
as a sign of love.
But I should mean it
most of all.

23

In the excitement of Connor asking me out again, I forget about the fireworks I'd caused recently and the fact that I'm grounded. I have no idea if Mom and Dad will ease up.

Eden and I spend the whole bus ride home talking about the winter formal—what we will wear, should we get our hair done, and how good the boys will look in suits. When I walk in the door at home, I see J.P. is home from college, heating up something in the microwave. He leans against the counter. "'Sup, String Bean?"

Hearing that makes me think back to all the fun, easy times we had before he left for college and I started growing up, and everything got complicated. I drop my backpack by the kitchen table and run into a hug with him, like I used to do when I was little.

"Aww, you miss me?" he rumples my hair and gently extricates himself from my arms so he can get his burrito. It's not the special kind Mom got from All-Mart's one-aisle pricey section with organic and allergy-friendly foods. "Or do you need something?" He takes a big bite.

"Just glad to see you. Guess you're free and clear of that whole celiac disease thing." My eyes dart to the burrito.

He nods and chews. "Yeah. Sorry about you. The Bean stands alone." As he passes me on his way to the couch he ruffles my hair again.

"Not really." I smile. Even if we're different, I have people. "Hey . . . when you were younger and got into trouble, did you ever get Mom and Dad to let up on grounding you?"

J.P. laughs. "Nope, not ever in the few times this saint was ever punished." He points at himself. "You're grounded? What'd you do?"

I can't look at him. "Ummm . . . ran away from Confirmation class and had a bad lunch with a boy."

Burrito chunks spray from his mouth. Then he chokes on a laugh. "Whoa. Guess I've been missing a lot. But that doesn't sound like you."

My shoulders sink. "I know. It's not, I don't think. I was feeling hurt. And I got angry. How come you never got angry?" I sit down on the couch a few inches away.

J.P. stops looking at the TV and faces me. "G.J., I'm a dude. I got angry plenty of times. But I always apologized and tried to make it better. Now, what's going on that makes you want to attempt a jailbreak?"

"The winter dance. This boy asked me to go with him in class today."

J.P.'s eyebrows go sky high. "A boy? The bad lunch boy?"

"Oh, no no *no*. Mom's met this kid. He goes to Confirmation classes at Sacred Heart. We've hung out before."

"Confirmation . . . that's right . . . that's all starting up for you. And two dates. Man, I *really* have missed a lot."

I giggle. "It wasn't a date. Just a bunch of us at the movies." Whenever J.P. calls home to talk to Mom and Dad, he and I just say "hey, how are you," lately. Is it weird to talk to him about this stuff?

J.P. chews thoughtfully. "Okay. As long as that's all it is. I want you to keep me posted. Maybe I should meet this kid."

"What?! No! Why?!"

"'Cuz as your older brother, I know what younger dudes might start thinking, and I want to make sure my li'l sis is protected." He pulls me into the crook of his elbow.

I wiggle out and chuck him on the shoulder. It's goofy, but nice that someone else is thinking of me. "Thanks, I guess?"

He chucks me back. "No prob. Hey. I know it's not really done, but you think maybe you might think about making me your Confirmation sponsor?"

I chew on that for a minute. Most of the girls in my class have already picked their sponsors—aunts, godmothers, older sisters, or girl cousins. But I don't have any of those. "Maybe. How 'bout we start with Facebook friends first? But it will have to wait until Christmas."

J.P. nods. "Deal."

* * *

When I open up my backpack the next morning, I find a present in one of the pockets. I eagerly unwrap it. It's a tube of light pink lip gloss. I look at the ingredients. No gluten. I'm about to throw away the wrapping paper when I see a note on the inside. "Happy early Christmas! For one of your presents, your father and I decided we will let you go to the winter formal—on one condition. J.P. chaperones. Love, Mom."

Before social studies class starts, I tell Connor I can go. We both smile big, my lips a *Pure Pink*.

Today is also my day to give my cultural history project. I'm about to start when Eden walks in with a huge tray covered in cloth. "Wait, wait, wait! You can't start without the refreshments!" Her eyes plead with Mr. Giopolous, who waves his hand in a "keep it quick" motion.

"What is that?" I whisper.

"It's challah! Gluten-*free* challah!" She whispers back. She sets it down on an empty desk and starts unwrapping it.

I rub my eyes and bite my glossed lips so I don't start crying right before this presentation. Evidence my friend is worth a million dollars: she knows just what to give.

I hastily shuffle my index cards around and start with a new introduction. On the fly, I say what I remember Eden telling me about challah this one time when I went to her place for dinner one Friday night. It was her Sabbath, she said. It's really cool to see everyone in class pass the tray from desk to desk and take a hunk of the braided bread like we did at the table. Everyone munches on it while I show the little Web page I built about bread.

There are giggles at our cooking experiments and funny sound effects from Eric when I had them play a countdown quiz on fun facts. Finally, I get to the part where I explain why I chose this topic. After interviewing Father Mazi, I now know why wheat.

The Catholic Church really wants to honor what Jesus did at the Last Supper—offering the wheat bread that becomes his Body. It wasn't some other food at the Last Supper, but definitely wheat bread and wine, which also have starring roles in many Gospel stories. And then earlier this week I finally found a really cool fact about wheat, which is maybe why Jesus chose to use it and not something else. I tell the class:

"Here's what's so special about wheat: each wheat berry actually hides a wheat germ. It just sits there inside the berry. You'd think that when the outer shell gets soft, cracks, and dies, the germ would die with it. But actually, it's an opportunity. The wheat germ still gets to grow. And eventually it becomes a new wheat plant."

Eden looks proud. Connor looks thoughtful. Gio looks like he might give me an A. Most of the class looks pretty puzzled.

"Wow. Bread. Huh. Anymore of that challah?" Eric says.

I can still taste the challah when I head into church for my third hour of adoration. To most of my classmates the biology of wheat is just some fun (not really) fact about bread. But I think I'm finally getting what I'm supposed to see. In Confirmation class we've been learning that God made our bodies a certain way for certain reasons. So why wouldn't God do the same thing when he was going to make the Eucharist? Jesus died and rose again. And like the wheat, we get a second chance to grow and become something new.

For the last Confirmation class before the holidays, we're having a shorter lesson and party. I walk in the door with my snack—a couple gluten-free cupcakes for me and the good stuff for everyone else. I was reading on this message board that some people just bake GF for everyone and everything, because it's easier, but honestly, I do not want to force that sludge on anyone's taste buds.

Ian comes in next. He's dressed liturgically for our last-class-of-the-season party. It's the third week of Advent, so dressed liturgically means this dusty rose sweater over a black shirt. He looks good. It makes me think of what Connor might wear tomorrow night at the dance. It's a good thing they aren't at the same school.

Julian's eye's bug out. "What are you wearing?"

"A sweater." Ian hands his Saran-wrapped tray of pigs-in-a-blanket to Miss Tompkins and sits down. Far away from Julian. And two people away from me.

Julian rolls his eyes. "Obviously. It's pink."

"Actually, I heard on this fashion podcast that pink used to be for men." I pop one of the pieces of safe caramel popcorn Paul and his sisters brought into my mouth. "It's in the red family, and red is a masculine color." I can't wait to tell Eden that one of the facts from her presentation is schooling this guy.

Ian smiles.

Julian's cheeks are bright red.

"Class, let's get settled." Mrs. Fermacelli starts to review everything we've talked about this semester.

I try to spend the class not looking at Ian. I have Connor I have Connor I have Connor I have Connor.

Well, okay, I don't have him. But he did make the first move by asking me to the winter formal. And I intend to keep my promise to go to the dance with him. I have a friend I have a friend I have a friend.

After we go through the fruits of the Holy Spirit one more time, the party begins. Hanna and Hallie make a game out of trying to make Julian smile. Instead, he starts talking to Nathan about getting picked to be an altar server at Midnight Mass. Paul and Ian are having a contest to see who can string the most popcorn the fastest. Angela comes over.

"I just want to say your dress is really pretty. Where did you get it?"

"Thanks!" I smooth out the skirt. "It's from Modelly."

"I *love* that store!"

"Really?"

She eagerly nods. "I don't get to go shopping much. It's just me and my Dad and my little sister. She's six."

I put a sympathetic hand on her shoulder. "I'm sorry. I didn't know."

She shrugs. "It's okay." She looks away for a second then blazes a smile at me. "Maybe we could go shopping tomorrow night!"

My whole body droops. "My school is having a dance tomorrow."

But her eyes sparkle. "Oh wow! How exciting. That's okay. Another time." She scoots closer. "So are you going with anyone?"

"I'm meeting a boy there. Connor Riley. He was at the retreat."

"Yeah! He was kinda quiet though, when he was there."

Her brow is furrowed. Oh boy. Does Angela think something is off with Connor? Of course, I remember every detail of the not-a-date date at the movies. He did say he didn't go to church very much and didn't get the point of Confirmation. Was his leaving the retreat really just out of concern for me, or also an excuse to take a break himself? Is it okay if we're not in the same place with the whole faith Thing?

I shrug. "But we're probably going to hang out with our friends most of the time." It's not a disaster that Connor and I won't be alone. Mrs. Fermacelli said if we're going to spend time in the company of boys, we should have a solid friend who knows stuff about chastity and will help us try to live it out. As Ms. Catholic Jeopardy, Angela definitely knows stuff. As a person, she definitely could be a friend.

"Hey . . . I know I can't do it tomorrow, but are you free Saturday? I placed in this design contest and next weekend my friend and I are going to the award ceremony at SoFash and then to Modelly. Want to meet us?"

Angela nods eagerly.

I smile. It's not even a disaster to call Olivia my friend. It feels right.

24

Friday is torture to get through. No one can concen-
trate. We're all thinking about the winter formal. Finally,
finally, the final bell rings. Instead of going home, I get
off the bus with Eden to escape Mom and the gazillion
pictures she'd want to take. As I slick my lips with the *Pure
Pink* gloss, Eden comes up beside me. We look at each
other, standing together again in front of the mirror. Eden
squeezes my side. She sighs a little.

"What?" I step my foot into a silver wedge.

She smiles. "Told you," and points to the mirror with
her head.

"Yeah." I squeeze her side back and put on the other shoe.

When we walk into the dance, I immediately spot Connor. He is in a dark blue suit and sports a silvery blue tie against a white shirt that looks like it's been ironed within an inch of its life.

"Hi," he breathes more than he says.

"Hi." I look at my feet.

A loud *squeeeee* interrupts the staring contest. "*Oh-em-gee!*" Melissa totters over in wine red heels. "Gloria Jean! You look *just* like Cinderella." She grabs my hands and spins me around. The skirt of my dress twirls and swirls like wisps of ocean.

On the last pivot, I go in for hug. When we release, I say, "Thanks. Now let's start having some fun before J.P. turns us *all* into pumpkins."

Connor whips his head around and makes a big show of scoping out for my brother. He's ladling some punch.

"Yes, ma'am," Connor chuckles. He extends the crook of his elbow and I reach to hold onto it.

For the next two hours, Connor and I spend a lot of time dancing to the fast, boppy songs a good foot away from each other. We awkwardly shuffle during a few slow songs. Zack and Eden, and Melissa and Eric do the same.

Halfway through the dance, there's a huge scene.

"Ugh! Get away from me, you creep!" Olivia is trying to worm out of Kyle's arms, which are trying to keep her dancing in a way that would have had J.P. marching me home. She runs toward the locker rooms. Kyle just runs his hand through his hair and goes to the punch table.

"Excuse me a minute, okay?" I follow Olivia.

Eden shoves her plate of snacks into Zack's hands. "Sorry boys. Girl group thing. Come on, Melissa."

The three of us peek our heads into the locker room. "Gimme just a minute first, okay?" I whisper. Eden nods.

Olivia sits on that rickety bench, stretches out her leg, and studies her foot. She lets out a long breath.

"*Wha-at*?" She doesn't look up.

I put my hand on her shoulder. "Just wanted to make sure you're okay."

She pulls her feet back in. "I'll be fine." She looks blankly at the hospital scrub green lockers in the corner.

"Okay. Just wanted to say that what you did was really smart."

Finally she looks at me. "Yeah?"

"Yeah!" I nod encouragingly.

She smiles. "Those guys are just . . ."

I lean back. "Guys? It's not just Kyle?" Oh no. Who else could it be?

Olivia rolls her eyes.

Back to her old self, I guess.

"Ding ding ding. You got it," she says. "Kyle's having this huge after party at the pool house and was telling Eric all about how 'safe' it will be because he stole those flash cards." She makes the air quotes. "Isn't that why you and your friends just ditched your dates?"

My stomach plummets. "Nooo. Maybe Eric—but—Zack and Connor wouldn't . . ."

Olivia tosses back her hair. "And what makes you so sure they wouldn't? I mean, do you *know* them, know them?"

I clamp my jaw shut. I honestly can't say. I get up with such force that the bench shakes. I yank open the locker room door and Eden and Melissa nearly tumble onto the floor. I lock the door behind them.

"What?" Eden breathes when she sees my face.

I cock my head at Olivia. "Tell them what you told me."

And so Olivia explains how Kyle and his new bro Eric are co-hosting an after party. At Kyle's "cabana." They are going to talk to Connor and Zack about getting us to all go and have some "low-risk" fun. More air quotes.

Melissa sinks to the bench. Eden kicks a locker with her heel. "Zack and I never . . . we," she sighs. "I would've thought we would've talked . . ."

I remain standing. I say a prayer. I breathe in and out. In and out. I may not know that much about Connor, but I know he doesn't love me yet, and I don't love him yet. But I need to find out some truth from the person himself.

"Well, I for one am not going to that party. And I'm going to run my mouth off." The girls just stand there, silent. But I clomp out of the locker room and down the gym floor in my little heels.

At the edge of the dance floor, Connor starts to smile that smile, but it stops short when the disco ball light dots pass over my face. Eric and Zack start to backwards walk toward the hall doors.

"No, you all stay. I think you *all* need to hear this." I stand right in front of them, the balls of my feet pressing down into my high heels. I am face to face with Connor. My shoes mean my lips are at the height of his lips.

"How could you?" Great. My strong voice has cracked

to let in a little whine. "I thought after that time at The Book Nook I could trust you. But then I hear about this party and the cards and . . ." by now my voice is thin and quiet. "How could you think I would ever do anything like that with you when we haven't even . . . kissed." I mouth the last word.

I finally break eye contact, not wanting him to see the tears pooling up. Eric seems to be inspecting his reflection in his shiny shoes. Zack puts his hands in his pockets and tries to walk away.

"What she said." Eden has come up behind me on my right side.

"Yeah." Melissa's on my left. She juts out her chin.

I put my arms around them. "What do you say we girls go and dance elsewhere?"

They smile, and arm in arm, we leave the boys with their mouths hanging open.

25

Soon, it's 11:00 and Eric and Zack have left. Eden
pouts, but Melissa reassures her they can talk in the morning. Olivia's older sister drives up. The windows are down
and some bumpy rap is thumping from the stereo. She
hangs out of the window to yell for Olivia. Half her chest
hangs out of her top. I see Olivia give a slight shake of her
head. I'm about to head back inside to wait for J.P. to finish
helping the teachers and chaperones clean up. Connor's
sitting on a ledge. He must still be waiting for his ride.

"Gloria Jean," he says in the softest voice imaginable.
Like this-is-my-confession soft. He eases himself off and

stands. "I am really sorry about the whole Kyle thing. I don't really know what I'm doing. While we were doing the presentation, I told Eric about you, and then he was all over me about what we might be doing. I guess Kyle's been in his head. I dunno." He shuffles his feet and looks at them. The brown boat shoes. "I've never been kissed either," he says all quiet.

My lips relax into a smile. "Join the club. We've got membership cards and T-shirts."

Connor looks up. "Designed by you?"

"Naturally!"

And then his right dimple moves higher up his cheek as he smiles *that* smile. And I feel ready to forgive him.

Connor inches toward me. Ohmygoodness. Is he going to kiss me? I want my eyes open. No! Closed. Wait. Do I even want to be kissed at all? Will there be more kisses after this one? There's no guarantee. What if next semester in Confirmation class I get to know Ian better and realize I'd rather be kissing him?

Connor rocks back and forth on his feet. "Well, good night." He leans forward a little.

My lips stay put.

My head nods.

A car horn beeps.

"That's my mom," he says.

I nod. My lips stay shut.

"I hope to see you again soon."

I nod and allow my lips to move—into a smile.

"Bye."

I wave.

My lips don't part.

✳ ✳ ✳

The next morning, I ask Mom if she wants to drop off the angel for our tree and crèche to be blessed at the church, and I can stop in, too. Do some adoration. She bounds from the couch. "Really? Is this something you really want to do? Or are you just trying to get your hours done early?" Her eyebrows scrunch together.

I smile at her. I am not faking anything today.

When we get there, I sign in and leave Mom to Mrs. Gomez. I head into the chapel. I'm the only one there, except for a head bowed down and a low voice praying something I don't recognize. A breeze comes through an open window. It smells like laundry. There *he* is.

I bless myself with holy water, bow, and then walk up the aisle. I get nervous for a second, wondering if I should go in the middle, or all the way up front, but definitely not where I can hear the guy. Or really, so he can't hear me.

I genuflect and then drop my other knee and stay on the cold tile floor like that for a moment. I close my eyes and then remember that's not the point. I should be looking.

I look right into Ian's long-sleeved rugby shirt.

"Gloria," he mouths.

I wave.

That hand of his rests on the back of the pew, so close to my hand that it tingles. He whispers so low I have to lean forward to hear him. "I was just saying these lyrics to this awesome song we heard at the retreat. And I realized you missed it and remembered how much you were into the songs we heard in class . . . and well, maybe during

187

the holiday break we can get together—if your parents are cool with it, of course—and talk about it, play it on my phone . . . there's this place called a dessert bar. . . ."

My head bobs up and down really fast. "Okay," he mouths. "Merry Christmas." His fingers linger and my heart tingles. I shrink into myself a little. I wave goodbye. He puts his thumb and pinky on the side of his face like it's a phone and points at me. "Tomorrow," he mouths. I smile.

And I turn around to look again, and I finally see. In the space where Ian was, at the front of the church, on the altar, is who I really came for. He is surrounded by this almost-snowflake-shaped halo on the altar. Sunlight bounces off one of the edges so the gold is gleaming. I squint to look harder at just him. Even though I've been here a few times, I still don't know if I'm saying the right things, and what more I can say. I could run through all the prayers I've ever learned. Gigi liked to say that the best prayer was his name. In my head, I try it. *Jesus.*

Suddenly, the last line of the song that Mrs. Fermacelli played a few weeks ago starts playing in my head on repeat. "Lead me to the truth and I will follow you with my whole life." I think that's what I've been wanting all along. To know what the truth is about love. And there's that Bible verse where Jesus says, "I am the Way, and the Truth, and the Life." So the song could also mean that I need to be led to Jesus. Well, here I am.

But this is just today. What does my whole life look like? It's for as long as I'm living, of course, but I think it also means with my whole heart and with each choice I make. And now that I've seen different sides, I think I know which way I'll go. All the guidelines I wanted to create for myself, how I thought the world should operate, don't make sense anymore, because I made them when I didn't know anything. And now? Now I'm still learning.

I thumb through the English missalette. I stop on a page that looks familiar. It's from a Gospel from John: "I give you a new commandment, love one another as I have loved you." I read over them. I draw a sharp breath. Of course. We've been given guidelines from the beginning. These rules from faith . . . these are rules of love. But not just any old sappy love, Love itself. And instead of judging a guy based on his ability to follow the commandments I've made up in my head, maybe he just needs to follow these. But who would do it best? I drop the missalette. It makes a dull thud as it flops against the kneeler and onto the floor. Instead of worrying about Connor or Ian, I should think of me.

I quickly look up at altar. My breathing is deep and slow and totally overshadowing any other noise in the place. I gaze for a long minute. Now I feel like it's okay to close my eyes. I feel like he's watching over me, with my head in his hands, softly kissing the top of it, like Dad did when I was little. I feel a smooth happiness—tingles—glide down through my head, wrap itself around my heart, and then all the way down until it fills up my feet.

In my head, I say the Our Father. When I get to "Give us this day, our daily bread," I smile.

I open my eyes and look up. My lips part, and I whisper, *Amen.* I believe.

Some Words About Celiac Disease

Hi! Thanks for sticking with me during this ginormous phase of my life. Principal Tourley told us on the first day of the 6th grade that these years were going to be full of changes. He had no idea.

Britt wanted to tell my story 1) because I kind of got into her head and she couldn't ignore me and B) her sister and little niece live with celiac—and are Catholic, just like me. So when I told her all I was learning about the disease and it matched with what her sister was saying—she knew she had to let others hear us.

You may have come across this scary statistic by some doctors who think as many as one in 141 people have celiac disease. That's not even like, half my 8th grade class. So I figured there's gotta be other kids with celiac out there. The part about all the extra homework I did when I got diagnosed was left out of this story. There are all kinds of posts on Internet forums about how other people got diagnosed, what symptoms they had, and how they felt. They were all. So. Different. One woman only found out because her dermatologist (skin doctor) couldn't figure out what was causing a rash.

Okay, so you might be reading this and then matching what's going with you and your stomach today or last Thursday and thinking—I HAVE CELIAC!

Uh. No. Well, maybe not. Celiac is an autoimmune disease, meaning it springs up in the body on its own rather than catching it from someone or somewhere else as a defensive reaction to something going very wrong. It can (but not always!) develop in people with certain risk factors. These factors (not the math kind), are things like having a parent, brother or sister, or even someone not in your immediate family, like grandparent or cousin who have celiac or another autoimmune condition like Type 1 diabetes.

If that's not you and you're still really worried, talk with your mom or dad (unless symptoms are so bad, they kinda already know something's wrong) and be sure to bring it up at your next regular doctor's appointment.

Hopefully many of you are in the clear! But remember—it's true what my dad said. Celiac can run in families. If you or a family member is diagnosed with it, everyone else in the family should talk with their doctor about getting tested. My brother J.P.'s bloodwork was negative, but because celiac is like a zit in that it can rear its ugly head at any time, he'll have to pay a little more attention to his body. There are also genetic tests he and my parents might have done to see what kind of threat level celiac poses them. For his sake, I hope it's none!

If you're curious about celiac disease or have it and want to learn more, here are some of the sites I found during the worst extracurricular homework ever:

Resources for Teens with Celiac

Celiac Disease Foundation: Teens and Young Adults—
http://www.celiac.org/index.php?option=com_content
&view=article&id=26&Itemid=46

CeliacSprue Association—http://www.csaceliacs.info/

CeliacTeen: Let Go of the Gluten blog—
http://celiacteen.com

National Foundation for Celiac Awareness—
http://www.celiaccentral.org

Teens Living with Celiac—http://teenslivingwithceliac.org
(They have a Catwalk for Celiac!)

Catholic Teens

Benedictine Sisters—http://www.benedictinesisters.org/
bread/low_gluten.php)

Catholic Celiac Children—http://catholicceliacchildren.
blogspot.com

Catholic Celiac Society—http://www.catholicceliacs.org/

Acknowledgements——

"The Thankful" Mysteries

I am blessed to reveal my gratitude for the wonderful people who helped bring Gloria Jean to life.

A heartfelt thank you to my parents, Robert and Phyllis Schlorff, who believed in me and that this day would come; to my sister Amy Schleicher, and her daughter Mallory, who inspired me to write Gloria Jean's story, and Charlie, Brandon, and Carleigh, for being the best brother-in-law and nephew and niece a girl could ask for; and to my twin, Bobby Schlorff, who would leave me alone enough so I could read and write.

A special thank you to my editor, Jaymie Stuart Wolfe, for her enthusiastic faith in me and my story, her incredible support, thoughtful edits, sage advice, and presence. With special gratitude to Sr. Mary Joseph Peterson for her beautiful design, and to Sr. Denise Benjamin and the whole Marketing team for introducing Gloria Jean to the world.

I am also so grateful for the prayers and support of Sisters Christina Wegendt, Emily Beata Marsh, Marlyn Monge, and Sean Mayer, and all the Daughters of St. Paul and staff of Pauline Books & Media who accompanied me on this journey.

And I hold deep appreciation for my kindred spirits in the book and writing worlds, especially Jo Knowles and Anna Stanisweski for their writing wisdom at Simmons College; Emily McLean and Shoshana Flax, who first met Gloria Jean and liked her; Carter Hasegawa and Jenna Brown for their friendship and book industry advice; the Newton Library SCBWI Writing Group; and all my Simmons pals.

And of course, I can't forget Chelsea Scheid, Divya Juturu, Erin Trowbridge, John-Michael Rouhana, and Linda Schwartz. Friends can be the greatest loves of our lives. Thank you for being mine.

I love you all.

About the Author

A Florida girl by birth, but Bostonian at heart, Britt Leigh lives and writes down the block from either cherry blossoms or snow, depending on the season. Working in the publishing business, she feels blessed to have a job where she can pray and play with prose. Her first writing for teens appeared in *Chicken Soup for the Soul's Teens Talk Middle School* and *Teens Talk Getting into College*.

Britt holds a certificate in catechesis from the Theological Institute for the New Evangelization at St. John's Seminary, a master of fine arts in writing for children from Simmons College, and two word-related degrees from the University of Florida (Go Gators!). When she's not immersed in writing, reading, talking, reviewing, or assisting books, she loves spending time with her 5 'Fs': faith, family, friends, football, and fancy. She once heard that authors are forever writing the same story over and over again. If that's true, her story is love. She blogs at brittleighbooks.com.

Catholic Fiction

Pauline Teen promises you stories that:

- ✍ reflect your life experience
- ✍ deal with tough topics
- ✍ take your questions seriously
- ✍ have a sense of humor
- ✍ don't talk at you, over you, or down to you
- ✍ explore living your faith in the real world

At Pauline, we love a good story and aspire to continue the long tradition of Christian fiction.* Our books are great reads. But they are also meant to engage your faith by accepting who you are *here and now* while inspiring you to recognize who God *calls you to become*.

*Think of classics like *The Hobbit, The Chronicles of Narnia, A Christmas Carol, Ben Hur,* and *The Man Who Was Thursday.*

Who: The Daughters of St. Paul

What: Pauline Teen—linking your life to Jesus Christ and his Church

When: 24/7

Where: All over the world and on www.pauline.org

Why: Because our life-long passion is to witness to God's amazing love for all people!

How: Inspiring lives of holiness through: Apps, digital media, concerts, websites, social media, videos, blogs, books, music albums, radio, media literacy, DVDs, ebooks, stores, conferences, bookfairs, parish exhibits, personal contact, illustration, vocation talks, photo... writing, editing, gra...

BOOKS & MEDIA

The Daughters of St. Paul operate book and media centers at the following addresses. Visit, call, or write the one nearest you today, or find us at www.pauline.org

CALIFORNIA
3908 Sepulveda Blvd, Culver City, CA 90230   310-397-8676
935 Brewster Avenue, Redwood City, CA 94063   650-369-4230
5945 Balboa Avenue, San Diego, CA 92111   858-565-9181

FLORIDA
145 SW 107th Avenue, Miami, FL 33174   305-559-6715

HAWAII
1143 Bishop Street, Honolulu, HI 96813   808-521-2731
Neighbor Islands call: 866-521-2731

ILLINOIS
172 North Michigan Avenue, Chicago, IL 60601   312-346-4228

LOUISIANA
4403 Veterans Memorial Blvd, Metairie, LA 70006 504-887-7631

MASSACHUSETTS
885 Providence Hwy, Dedham, MA 02026   781-326-5385

MISSOURI
9804 Watson Road, St. Louis, MO 63126   314-965-3512

NEW YORK
64 West 38th Street, New York, NY 10018   212-754-1110

PENNSYLVANIA
Philadelphia—relocating   215-676-9494

SOUTH CAROLINA
243 King Street, Charleston, SC 29401   843-577-0175

VIRGINIA
1025 King Street, Alexandria, VA 22314   703-549-3806

CANADA
3022 Dufferin Street, Toronto, ON M6B 3T5   416-781-9131